Relentless Pursuit

Kathleen Brooks

An original work of Kathleen Brooks.

Relentless Pursuit
Copyright @ 2013 by Kathleen Brooks

All Rights Reserved. No part of this book may be used or reproduced in any manner whatsoever without written permission, except in the case of brief quotations embodied in critical articles and reviews.

This book is a work of fiction. The names, characters, places, and incidents are products of the writer's imagination or have been used fictitiously and are not to be construed as real. Any resemblance to persons, living or dead, actual events, locale, or organizations is entirely coincidental.

ISBN: 1484858913
ISBN-13: 9781484858912

Cover art provided by Calista Taylor.
http://www.calistataylor.com

Books by Kathleen Brooks

Bluegrass Series

Bluegrass State of Mind
Risky Shot
Dead Heat

Bluegrass Brothers

Bluegrass Undercover
Rising Storm
Secret Santa: A Bluegrass Series Novella
Acquiring Trouble
Relentless Pursuit

Acknowledgment

A special thank you to Yasmin Gonzalez of Vohne Liche Kennels for her professional insight into police and military K-9 handling. I was so impressed with Yasmin's experience and all that Vohne Liche does to help protect our police officers and military through the positive training of their dogs.

PROLOGUE

Two Years Ago...

Pierce Davies sat back in the chair and held his breath. He looked down at what he had just finished and then at his professor. Dr. Howard Oldham was staring similarly at the object sitting on the tile floor of lab 107 in the University of Kentucky Agricultural Building. The silence of the early morning was thundering in his ears as he pulled out his smartphone.

"Okay, here it goes." Pierce pressed in a series of commands and waited. The object on the floor turned on. The red light turned to green as the object started to move across the floor.

"You did it, Pierce!" Dr. Oldham shouted as they followed the object down the darkened hall.

Pierce worried as the object stopped by a ficus tree to test it. "I don't know yet. I still think it's too soon to celebrate." Pierce paused and flashed a smile to Dr. Oldham. "But I sure as hell am excited."

"We need to test it out in the environment first," Dr. Oldham said, more to himself as he nodded his gray head and pushed his black-rimmed glasses back up his rounded nose.

Pierce put his hand on his hips and narrowed his hazel eyes as the object started moving again. "I know the perfect place, Dr. Oldham. There's an abandoned farm in Keeneston.

Relentless Pursuit

The owner died and a family member who owns it lives out of state. I've had my eye on it since I was eighteen. Now I just need a loan."

"That I can help with. I know a guy." Dr. Oldham winked as his bushy eyebrows bounced. His smile slipped and his lips tightened. "You know what this means if this works?"

Pierce nodded. He may be the baby of the family, but he also might have just invented something that would change the farming community forever. His brothers never seemed to realize that he was an adult after they came home from the Special Forces, showing off their talents. Pierce was always paying attention, even if being the youngest somehow made him invisible.

He had learned hand-to-hand combat from his oldest brother, Miles, during their workouts together. He had paid close attention to Marshall when he interned at his old security company and learned all kinds of neat tricks from assessing risk to lock picking. Then he learned the computer skills it took to hack into nearly any system in the world from Cade, the youngest of the three brothers who were deployed. From that knowledge, Pierce worked backwards and became somewhat of an excellent programmer. Cade had never thought twice in pulling out the computer to hack into some database for the U.S. government when they called, even though Pierce was sitting there on the couch watching football.

He loved his brothers, all four of them, and his sister, who was probably the only one who saw his potential. But for some reason he wanted to keep this discovery from them. It was his and he wasn't ready to share it with anyone until it was so perfect that Cade couldn't hack it, Marshall couldn't disable it, and Miles couldn't find any fault in its design.

Pierce tapped a button on his cell phone and the object turned around and rolled back into the classroom and shut itself off. "Let's not get ahead of ourselves. We'll test it, make adjustments, and then test it again. It'll take a little while longer, but when it's perfect..." Pierce looked up at his professor. "We can't tell *anyone*. Not your wife, not Aiden, no one. Not even my family."

Dr. Oldham nodded his head and held out his hand. Pierce shook it and the two men slapped each other on the back. "I just can't believe we did it! If this works…"

"I know. I can't really believe it myself." Pierce pulled out the flash drive from his computer with all his notes and programming code and placed it in his pocket. He gathered the six notebooks in front of him and shoved them into his backpack. "Now all I need is the deed to that land."

CHAPTER ONE

Present day...

Tammy slid the hanger across the old metal rail in the closet and sighed. Too teenage-y. Too old. Too boring. Ugh! She knew she had the perfect dress to debut the new Tammy Fields to the world tonight at the social event of the year. Miles and Morgan were getting married in the most talked about wedding Keeneston had ever seen since Dani married Mo, a real life prince, and she just needed to find that special dress in her closet.

Tammy pushed aside the sweater she had worn when Cy Davies kissed her and changed her life on Christmas Eve. She was just about to give up hope of ever finding love when the sexy Santa grabbed her and planted one on her right in front of the whole town—and right in front of his brother Pierce. It was then she realized that she was tired of being "cute little Tammy." So she had marched all five-foot-one inches of herself into paralegal classes the following week with a new attitude. It took some convincing but she repeated it enough that she started to believe it. She was smart. She was sexy. And she could do anything if she put her mind to it.

She improved her grades so much that she graduated earlier this month with honors. As a reward, her boss, Henry Rooney, gave her a promotion. Tammy was now no longer just a secretary at his defense law firm, but his new paralegal. With the promotion came a much-needed raise from both Henry and McKenna Mason Ashton, the other attorney who shared office space with them. McKenna, or Kenna to all her friends, had even taken her out for a celebratory dinner at a fancy restaurant in Lexington.

With her first increased paycheck, Tammy hit the stores in Lexington. Instead of jeans or a miniskirt, Tammy was now wearing sexy pencil skirts and fitted blouses to work. Once known for her ever-changing hair color, Tammy started growing her hair out into a sleek ear-length bob with edgy sweeping bangs. Gone were her pink highlights and, in return, her naturally light-blonde hair shined.

As she stepped out of the salon, she ran smack into the Greek god who ran the restaurant near her paralegal school. She had flattened her hands against a ripped abdomen and looked up into the bluest eyes she'd ever seen. His wavy, long black hair was shoved behind his ears and he wore a smile that caused her to blink twice. When he said, "Excuse me," Tammy felt herself starting to melt. His smooth accented voice enveloped her and she almost leapt into his arms until she remembered she was the new Tammy.

"Pardon me, it was entirely my fault," she had said with a glint in her misty blue eyes.

"Don't you go to school near my restaurant? I seem to remember you studying while you ate lunch."

"Yes, I did. But I graduated and I'm now a paralegal at a law firm in Keeneston," Tammy had said rather proudly.

"Well then, we must celebrate your success. Let me take you out to lunch." He had grinned and Pierce's sexy smile became a distant memory for Tammy.

Demetri bought her lunch and she had never felt so empowered as to be sitting there having an adult discussion about careers and interests. She only faltered when he asked where she lived. Tammy had never been embarrassed about her upbringing in Keeneston Park, the local mobile home community, but she no longer felt as if it defined her. Instead she felt as if she finally had the courage to embark on something new.

She finished lunch with Demetri and left with his phone number in hand and a new mission. Tammy headed straight to the Blossom Café in downtown Keeneston. Not only was it the center of the town and the place to eat with a generous side of gossip, it also held the key to her future.

Tammy could feel her stronger, more confident self rising to the surface and she was ready to embrace it. She was no longer the overly perky, sex-crazed girl of her past. However, in her defense, the only man she had literally tried to jump was Ahmed, and who wouldn't want to jump dark, dangerous, and drop-dead gorgeous Ahmed?

Tammy marched into the Blossom Café with her shoulders back and promptly begged Miss Daisy and Miss Violet to let her rent the apartment upstairs. In just one day, she moved all of her things from her rented mobile home and into the apartment above the café. She decorated the place with pride and hung her diploma on the wall. With her hands on her hips, she decided then and there that Pierce Davies had missed out on a good thing.

She had been pining over him for two years and that was two too many. So what if he was a sweet, sexy cowboy? So what if he was tall with brown hair streaked with blonde highlights, the kind that made you want to run your hands through? And so what if he had hazel eyes you could get lost staring into? If he didn't—rather couldn't—see her for the woman she was, then out with the old and in with the Demetri! Tammy had picked up the phone and called Demetri right then. The last couple of weeks had been wonderful. Real dates with a man who saw her for the woman she was and not the kid she had been. There was only one problem with Demetri that she had discovered… he wasn't Pierce.

Tammy shoved the hanger down the rod and smiled when she finally found the dress she was looking for. Tonight was Miles and Morgan's wedding and she was going to bring this whole strange love triangle to a head. One way or another, at the end of the night she'd either have Pierce or move on from him once and for all.

Pierce Davies stood at the front of Saint Frances Church and smiled as all of his family's friends took their seats in the pews. He gave a wink to his date, Jasmine, and also sent a killer smile to Summer, the part-time waitress at the café. They had gotten the five-minute warning from Father James and paraded out to the front of the church to await Morgan's arrival. Miles was standing tall and proud, waiting to be brought to his knees by the sultry Morgan.

Quite honestly, Pierce was disappointed in his brothers. There was nothing wrong with marriage, but they had all fallen hard and fast into the husband role. Thanks, but no thanks. He was twenty-seven, not thirty-six like Miles. Now it was just he and Cy as the remaining Davies bachelors. He looked at Jasmine, the president of the Keeneston Belles, and smiled when she blew him a kiss. It did have its rewards being the last man standing, which he was since Cy was nowhere to be found since Christmas.

Pierce heard the murmurs and whispers from the crowd and turned to see what the gossip was about. Tammy Fields had just walked in. He knew Tammy had a crush on him. Shoot, the whole town knew. Tammy was about as subtle as a freight train. But, he wasn't ready for the commitment she deserved, and she was too much of a spitfire to deserve anything but full attention. Pierce acknowledged he was in a rebellious, have-fun-date-as-many-women-as-you-wanted stage and he didn't even want to think about dating Tammy yet. Father James even said a prayer for it before they came out just now. Cade had asked, "Why didn't he just take her out on a date?" Well, because Tammy would be the woman chasing him down the street with a frying pan when she found out they weren't dating exclusively.

"She'd be a wonderful girlfriend," a voice from the back of his head told him. And he had hated seeing her with Cy... but you married that girl, you didn't date and dump her. And the *marriage* word was strictly forbidden in his vocabulary. Although, he had to secretly admit every now and then, he'd thought about that one little word. Just not yet, though! He'd keep his distance until he was ready to devote himself. For now he was enjoying

Jasmine. Jas was a knockout with breasts that he could get lost in and curves that were well worth the ride.

Pierce looked away from Jasmine's ample assets and back down the aisle just in time to see one of Miles's Ranger buddies sit down. It was then that he was afforded his first real look at Tammy. He felt his eyes go wide as she stood looking nothing like the Tammy he had gotten to know these last couple of years. Gone was the pink hair. Gone were the clothes of an eighteen-year-old. And gone was the innocent look on her face.

Pierce was in awe of the reinvented Tammy, but not with the six-foot-one Greek with his paws all over her. And what was she wearing? The little black dress crisscrossed over her pert breasts before the neckline plunged to her tight stomach. A gold necklace hung around her neck and disappeared into the depths of cleavage he didn't even know she had. Pierce's eyes traveled down the tight dress to where it ended at her knees. Her bare legs were put on display by sky-high red heels. He'd never seen anything so damn sexy in his life.

Pierce felt his hand tighten into a fist and his eyes narrow. Sure, he wasn't dating her, but that didn't mean someone else got to! Before he knew it, Morgan was walking down the aisle, but he couldn't tear his eyes away from where the Greek bastard was resting his hand on her knee. Did she think she would be able to get away with this kind of behavior? He couldn't wait for this ceremony to be over so he could have a few words with her.

The reception was in full swing when Pierce was finally able to stop smiling for pictures. He hurried through his parents' house and into the backyard that had been transformed into a romantic starry night-themed reception. He paused and looked around until he found her dancing on the floor with her date. The dancing stopped as Miles and Morgan were introduced to the cheering crowd. Now was his chance to confront Tammy. Another dance was going to start and he saw that her new guy had headed to the bar.

Pierce weaved in and out of the crowd until he found Tammy watching his brother and Morgan share their first dance. "Tammy,

Relentless Pursuit

we need to talk." Pierce put his hand on her arm and felt its smoothness under his rough hands.

"Hi, Pierce! Don't you look dapper? I'm glad you're here. I want to introduce you to Demetri. He's just gone off to get me some wine." Tammy smiled up at him. "Demetri is competing in a triathlon next month. Isn't that something? I thought you might like to hear about it. I know you like to run, but I don't know if you enjoy the other aspects of a triathlon."

Pierce smirked. "Triathlons are for sissies. If you want a rush, try riding a bull that's intent on killing you. But we have more important things to talk about."

Tammy's brow furrowed in confusion as she continued to look up at him. Dammit. She was such a contradiction. She was all sweet and caring, but in this outfit she was a commanding siren. "What's so important, Pierce?" she asked in that sweet Southern voice of hers.

"What do you think you're doing bringing that guy here?" he accused not so tactfully. But he was angry and ignored his harsh tone.

"Morgan said I could bring a date. Why do you care?" Tammy snapped sharply. "You're here tonight with Jasmine, right?"

Pierce watched as she crossed her arms under her chest and he felt like groaning. That dress was going to be the death of him. "I don't care about her! I'm just enjoying myself. And I care because you shouldn't be with someone like that. He's only here to get laid." Pierce felt his jaw tighten as he thought about that man with his hands on her.

"Funny, I'm also here to enjoy myself and get laid. See, no problem after all, but thanks for looking out for me," she said with a shrug of her bare shoulders and a little smirk on her face.

"No, you are not. You aren't getting laid tonight or any other night, thank you very much. If you're going to get laid, then it'll be by me, dammit, and no one else." Pierce felt his face heat up, but he was too angry to stop his posturing. Maybe he should've thought this out better.

"Oh no you aren't. You had that chance for two years but you blew it repeatedly by ignoring me and choosing other women over me. What did you expect, that I'd spend the rest of my life sitting at home pining over you?" She stood ramrod straight and stared him down.

Pierce's mind went blank and so he said the only thing he could think of, "Well, yes."

"You're an idiot, Pierce, and you just confirmed that I made the right choice with Demetri. Excuse me, I'm going to go dance with my date." Tammy turned her head and walked off.

Pierce was sure she was swinging her hips just to irritate him further. Pierce cursed under his breath as he saw Demetri slide his hand around her tiny waist and lead her out to the dance floor. He felt someone come to stand next to him and knew it was his sister before he even looked over at her.

"You know I love you, right?" Paige Davies Parker asked as she bounced her son, Ryan, on her hip. Her shoulder length brown hair was swept up into a fancy style and she glowed in the one shoulder gown she was wearing.

"Yes," Pierce answered hesitantly. Where was his sister going with this?

"Normally you're so empathetic, but you were too harsh this time and shoved her right into his arms. Very poorly done, Pierce." Paige left him standing there watching as Demetri guided Tammy to the dance floor.

When Demetri's hand slid down her waist and rested on the round curve of her bottom, he let loose with another curse and turned toward the bar. The only thing that was going to get him through tonight was to drown his sorrow and stupidity in a bottle of bourbon.

CHAPTER TWO

Pierce groaned as the bright morning light tried to penetrate his eyelids. Everything hurt. Everything was pounding. His head was spinning and his face was throbbing. God, how much did he have to drink last night? A better question when he could finally open his eyes—where was he? And why was he on his stomach in something wet?

"Get up! Get up! Aw, that's a good bird."

Ah, so he was at home. He bet Paige dragged his drunken ass home last night. Gus, his blue-fronted Amazon parrot continued to squawk until Pierce opened his eyes. Everything spun and he slammed them shut before he could even get his eyes fully open.

"Shut up, Gus," Pierce mumbled into the floor.

"Get up! Get up!" Gus squawked again. Okay, that was it. He was going to get up and throw a cover over his cage and then crawl into bed and spend the day nursing a hangover.

Pierce tried to roll over and felt pain shoot through his side so he gave up and lay back down on his stomach. What on earth had happened when he was drinking? He felt as if he'd been beaten up. Oh no! Had he gotten into it with Demetri? Why couldn't he remember?

Pierce slowly opened the eye that hurt less and used his hand to block out the morning light. As his vision focused, he realized it wasn't the morning light that had woken him up, but his lamp had been knocked over and was shining right in his eyes. He shoved the intrusive light away and slowly pushed up onto his elbows and looked around his house.

"What the..." Pierce held up his hand into the light and saw the blood dripping from his wrist and falling into the pool of blood on the floor beneath him. "Jesus!" Pierce scrambled back and hit something hard.

He ignored the pain shooting through his body as he spun around to see what he had run into. Lying next to him was the bloodied and battered body of Dr. Oldham. "Doc!" Pierce scrambled forward and felt for a pulse. There was none, but that didn't stop him from starting CPR.

Pierce's head spun, but he pushed the blackness and the cobwebs clouding his mind away. He leaned forward and started chest compressions. He needed an ambulance immediately. Looking around his house for the first time, he saw that it was a disaster.

His lamp was on the floor. Pictures knocked from the wall and his coffee table was smashed. His baseball bat lay near the front door and he felt his stomach start to recoil. Now he knew what happened to Dr. Oldham. Pierce continued CPR, he'd look for his cell phone in just a minute.

Pierce gave one last chest compression and then sat up to pat down the pockets of his torn tuxedo to look for his cell phone when the front door was shattered in. He dove away from the door and tried to leap to his feet, but a gun was in his face before he could move.

"Lexington police! On the ground! On the ground, right now!" someone shouted from behind a raised rifle.

"Help him!" Pierce screamed as he was shoved to the ground. "Please, help him! He needs an ambulance!"

"On the ground! Hands behind your head or I will shoot you!" A S.W.A.T. officer jammed his knee into Pierce's back and pulled his arms painfully behind him until they were encased in steel cuffs.

"Aw, that's a bad bird, that's a bad bird!" Gus squawked as he flapped his wings in agitation as the officers stormed past his cage.

Pierce looked frantically around as people flooded his small house. He could hear them calling for EMTs and then he took a breath when he saw Cole, Annie, and Marshall standing at the front door.

"Marshall! What's going on? What happened?" Pierce called out. If anyone knew what was going on, it would be his brother, the local sheriff.

"Pierce Davies, you're under arrest for the murder of Howard Oldham. You have the right to remain silent…" the officer who just cuffed him started as Pierce was yanked to his feet.

"Marsh?" Pierce asked frantically.

"Just don't say anything, dammit." Marshall's jaw was tight as he watched Pierce being dragged out the door. "The only words you need to say are that you invoke your right to counsel and want your attorney. I'm calling Henry now."

Marshall pulled out his cell phone, but Pierce wasn't allowed to talk anymore. He was shoved into the back of a cruiser and the door slammed shut. His head spun, his heart pounded, red and blue lights flashed. What the hell had just happened? This had to be a dream.

Pierce looked out the window at his brother arguing with the detective in charge. He could hear Marshall asking to ride along with his brother, but his plea was shot down immediately. Cole, the Special Agent in Charge of the Lexington FBI office and Pierce's brother-in-law, put his hands on his hips and narrowed his silver eyes under his black cowboy hat in a move Pierce recognized from when Cole stood his ground with Paige. Annie, Pierce's sister-in-law who was married to Cade, was a retired DEA agent and a current deputy in Keeneston. She tried next but was similarly rejected from accompanying Pierce to the police station. Pierce was pretty sure he saw steam coming out from under Annie's red hair as she glared at the detectives.

The police detective turned his back to Pierce and spoke to Marshall. "Look, I appreciate you letting us come into your jurisdiction, but we have a murder and possible kidnapping to investigate. You gave us permission to enter your jurisdiction when Mrs. Oldham filed her missing person report and we tracked Dr. Oldham's phone to this location. You granted us the authority to investigate in your county and while I thank you for that, I can't let a sheriff, an FBI agent, or a former DEA agent ride along with my suspect to feed him information that could hinder our investigation. Especially when there is such a blatant conflict of interest! I'm sorry, but due to that conflict, the Lexington PD will be running this investigation alone."

Pierce rested his head against the cold window and closed his eyes. "Wake up. It's time to wake up," he repeated until the door to the cruiser was opened.

"Time to go. Detective Cowell, you take the suspect," the other detective said as he started to drive away. Pierce watched as his brother and family grew smaller and smaller in the distance.

"Do you understand these rights as I have read them to you?" the tough-as-nails young detective asked him.

"I do."

Marshall cursed and kicked the ground. He turned to his brother and sister-in-law in complete confusion. "What just happened? Pierce couldn't have killed someone, could he?"

"You know he didn't, Marshall!" Annie shot back to him, her agitation clear in her voice.

"The best thing to do now is to call Henry and get him to the police station before they start interrogating him. He looked out of it and I don't know if I trust him to remember to keep his mouth shut." Cole said as he placed his hands on his hips and surveyed the ongoing crime scene investigation.

Marshall took a deep breath. "You're right. I'll call him now." Marshall dialed the number and waited while it rang and rang. He cursed again when Henry's voicemail picked up. "He's not answering. Dammit!"

"Call Tammy. She might know where he is," Annie suggested as she scrolled through her phone for Tammy's cell. "Here you go."

Marshall dialed Tammy's number and waited. It rang and he held his breath willing Tammy to pick up the phone.

"What?" a tiny sleepy voice said over the line.

"Thank God! Tammy, it's Marshall. Pierce has been arrested by the Lexington police for murder and we can't get hold of

Henry!" Marshall half-screamed into the phone. He'd been cool under fire while on tours of duty with the Special Forces, but nothing shook him more than his family in trouble. His little brother was being interrogated and thrown behind bars, and there was nothing he could do to protect him.

"What? This isn't funny, Marshall." Tammy's soft voice turned hard and Marshall got worried she'd hang up.

"It's not a joke. I've tried to get hold of Henry, but he's not answering." Marshall took a deep breath and tried to contain his frustration.

"Okay, I'll hurry to the police station. You go to Henry's and beat on the door. He went home last night with one of the Belles. I couldn't tell which one. They all look the same to me. I'll meet you at the station."

Before Marshall could respond, Tammy had hung up the phone. "Annie, get over to Henry's and drag his ass out of bed. I have to go tell my parents what's happened." Marshall slid into his cruiser with a sense of dread. How was he going to tell his parents that their baby was in jail for killing a man?

Tammy leapt out of the bed and crashed to the floor, her feet tangled in the sheets. Her heart was pounding and her mind was a runaway train. What had happened? Who had Pierce killed? But, Pierce couldn't have killed anyone! She yanked her black suit out of the closet, shoved her feet into some heels, and ran out the door with her car keys.

She floored her twelve-year-old Honda Civic and made it to Lexington in record time. Tammy pulled into a parking space at the police station and paused when her cell phone rang. She looked at the caller ID and sighed in relief.

"Henry! Where are you?"

"I'm with Annie. We're less than ten minutes away." Henry's confident voice calmed her as she strode to the front door.

"I'm here. What do I do?"

"Identify yourself to the front desk. Tell them you're from the law firm representing Pierce Davies and are here based on Pierce's request. Don't let them sit you in the waiting area. Demand to see him immediately."

"Got it." Tammy squared her shoulders and pushed through the door.

Pierce couldn't get used to the cold steel around his wrists. His hands were still in cuffs as he sat at the worn and dented table in the interview room. He could see his reflection in the two-way mirror—well, most of it anyway. One of his eyes was swollen shut and he was still so dizzy it was hard to focus on the two detectives sitting across from him.

The younger one, Detective Cowell, was playing bad cop. He was trying to intimidate Pierce with his size and hard looks. Too bad for him Pierce wasn't falling for it. He grew up with Miles. That sort of posturing and mean looks didn't have any effect on him. The older detective introduced himself as Basher and was trying to play the friend card.

"You'll be lucky if you ever see the light of day again, Davies," Cowell sneered.

"Maybe it was self-defense. If you cooperate with us, I'll make sure the D.A. goes easy on you, what do you say?" Basher asked with a soft, pleasant voice in stark contrast to Cowell.

"I say what I've said before. I want my attorney and I'm not saying a word until I speak with him. Aren't you supposed to stop questioning me now?" Pierce was starting to get angry. He had tuned out the detectives and was thinking about Dr. Oldham.

"That's fine. We won't ask you a single question." Cowell turned to Basher. "You know, I bet the D.A. may even consider the death penalty for murdering a beloved professor."

If Pierce's eye weren't swollen shut, he would've rolled it. A noise from the hall drew his attention instead. He could hear raised voices and then all of the sudden the door to the interview room burst open. His good eye went wide as he saw Tammy shove her way past an officer and into the room.

"I'll arrest you if you take one more step!" the officer yelled at her.

"What is the meaning of this? You're interfering with an interrogation, young lady." Detective Cowell shot to his feet and glowered at Tammy.

Pierce watched in amazement as Tammy's big round blue eyes narrowed and her hands moved to her hips. "Interrogation? Really? Has he requested an attorney? Because I'm positive he did."

Tammy strode aggressively up to Detective Cowell and ran a skeptical eye over him before turning to Pierce. "Pierce, don't you say one word. And you, what's your name?" she asked, turning back to Detective Cowell.

"I'm Detective Randy Cowell, and who might you be so I know the name to put on the arrest papers?" Detective Cowell smirked down at her.

"Don't you dare patronize me, detective. I'm the person who will have you brought up on charges if you don't get Mr. Davies medical attention at once! It is clear that he is severely injured and yet you have denied him access to a doctor." Tammy pointed a finger right at Detective Cowell.

"Okay, calm down everyone." Detective Basher held up his hands. "We'll arrange transport to the hospital, but we'll be back in just a minute and then we want some answers."

Pierce waited quietly as the detectives left the room. He wanted to jump up and hug Tammy. She was an avenging angel; all she had needed was a sword to complete the picture.

"Tammy," Pierce started.

"Not one word, Pierce. I bought you a couple of minutes. Henry and Annie will be here in five minutes. Then they'll be forced to take you to the hospital and to give you some time with Henry." Tammy bent down in front of him and took his face in her hands. "Gosh almighty, you look as if you were run over by a truck… twice."

"It feels as if I were," Pierce mumbled as he leaned into Tammy's soothing touch.

Pierce raised his head when the door was opened. Henry came in with the detectives trailing close behind.

"Jesus, he needs a doctor at once!" Henry boomed.

"We're ready to take him at anytime. Do you want a couple minutes with him before the officer takes him?" Detective Basher asked unhappily.

"Yes. Leave us and turn off the cameras and voice recordings. I'll knock on the door when we're ready, and take off my client's cuffs." Henry didn't say another word until the cuffs were removed and there was a soft rap on the two-way mirror indicating the video was now off.

"Pierce, what happened?"

"I don't know!" Pierce ran his hand over his head and stopped at the sore spot on the back of his head. "I've been sitting here trying to remember from the second I opened my eyes and found myself at my house. Nothing. Just a big black spot in my memory."

"Calm down, Pierce. It'll be okay. We'll talk to the doctor and see what she says. Marshall called Noodle and he already notified Emma, Dr. Francis that is, and she'll be waiting to examine you."

"Henry, do they really think I murdered Dr. Oldham? He was my friend. I have no reason to murder him."

"Yes, they do," Henry said solemnly. "They will run the DNA evidence they took from your person when they arrested you and are sure it'll match up to the DNA evidence found on Dr. Oldham. Further, you have defensive marks on your body and the murder weapon is your baseball bat found in your house, which will undoubtedly have your prints on it."

"I know the DNA evidence will clear me," Pierce said, more to himself than to Henry and Tammy.

"You think it will. But since you can't remember, we don't know if it will. The DNA test will come back within ten days and then we'll have our answer. But for now you are the only suspect," Henry told him.

"What I don't understand is how the police ended up at my place." Pierce said as he started pacing across the tiny room.

"That's another problem. Annie told me in the car that there was a 9-1-1 call made. Since Dr. Oldham placed the call from his cell phone out in the county, the state police answered it out of Frankfort," Henry explained. "The trouble is on the tape Dr. Oldham says, 'I've dialed the police. There's no point in killing me. They'll be here any minute.' Then you can hear sounds of a fight and the line goes dead. Frankfort traced the phone's owner to Dr. Oldham. When they came across a missing person's report just filed in Lexington, they called the Lexington police. The Lexington Police Department got in touch with Mrs. Oldham, who told them her husband had failed to come home from the lab the night before. With her permission, the cops used the GPS in Dr. Oldham's phone to track the location."

"Oh my God. Now I'm even starting to think I did it." Pierce buried his head in his hands and sighed. A feeling of despair washed over him so strong it almost stole his breath.

There was a knock on the door and Annie peeked in. "I'm sorry to interrupt, but the police transport to the hospital is ready."

"Okay then. Let's get you patched up," Tammy tried to say cheerfully, but it fell flat.

Two officers came in and put the blasted cuffs back on his wrists. Pierce saw the worry and fear in his friends' eyes. Things weren't looking good for him. There was no way he would've killed Dr. Oldham, was there?

CHAPTER THREE

Pierce was escorted into an exam room and handcuffed to the hospital bed. The two officers stood on each side of the bed and waited for his doctor to arrive. Soon enough the bouncing brown curls of Dr. Francis made their way into the room. Her head was down as she looked at a chart in her hands.

"Mr. Davies, it looks as though you've been in a bit of trouble. Let's check you over and see what we can find." Dr. Francis raised her head finally and looked at the full room. "Officers, please uncuff Mr. Davies and then step out into the hall."

"I'm sorry, ma'am, but we can't do that. This man is under arrest for murder."

"I know that. But I need him to do tests that require the use of his arms and hands. You can stay out in the hall. I doubt Mr. Davies will hurt me and I'll only be a scream away if he does. So, please, uncuff him. Thank you," she said in a tone that didn't broker argument.

Pierce waited for the cuffs to be removed as Dr. Francis pulled out a white robe. "Here, take off your clothes and put this on." Dr. Francis tossed the robe on the bed and turned to have a word with the officers. "I'm going to need to do X-rays and maybe even an MRI. You can escort us. I'll let you know when we're ready to go."

Pierce hissed as he reached to take off his shirt and Dr. Francis turned to see what movement caused the pain. "Where is it hurting, Pierce?" she asked kindly, now that the officers were gone.

"Everywhere." Pierce mumbled as he gave up trying to slide out of his dress shirt.

"Here, let me help you." Dr. Francis gave a small cluck as she saw the bruises developing on his side and across his abdomen. "Lie back, this might hurt." She felt along his rib cage and Pierce was worried he'd pass out from pain.

"I can't quite tell if any are broken, but they're either fractured or severely bruised. There are hematomas all around your midsection as if you were beaten. A couple days being wrapped tight will help. What happened?"

"That's the main problem. I don't remember. Please, Doc, help me be able to remember so I can prove my innocence," Pierce pleaded.

"I don't know if I can, but let's see what I can find. From what I gathered from the police, they think they have you dead to rights." Dr. Francis ran her hand down his arms and checked his hands. "Interesting."

"What?" Pierce asked as he looked down at his hands.

"There's no swelling of the knuckles," she murmured as she moved on to his face and head.

"So?"

"Even if you were a seasoned fighter, there would be some swelling to evidence punches had been thrown. It appears that you either didn't throw a single punch while being beaten, which I find hard to believe, or you were incapacitated and unable to throw a punch. Ah, here, on the back of your head."

"Yeah, I felt that earlier. It hurts like the devil."

"It's also incredibly swollen. It looks like this knock to the head is probably the cause of your memory loss. I'm going to draw some blood for a blood alcohol test, but I think we can go ahead and assume it's going to show you are still intoxicated. Let me take some pictures. This will help you in court if you need them." Dr. Francis pulled out a camera from the drawer and snapped some shots of his hands and the back of his head. She also documented the injuries on his abdomen by measuring the bruises and photographing them.

"Will my memory come back?" Pierce worried.

"Maybe. It's hard to tell. Head wounds are very tricky. My best guess, and I should be able to confirm with an MRI, is that you have swelling in your brain from this blow to the head. Once your brain recovers and the swelling goes down, I think that some of your memories will come back."

"What do we do to get the swelling down?" Pierce grimaced as Dr. Francis examined the injury again.

"Not too much. I can give you some anti-inflammatories. However, time is the best healer. For now, let's get that MRI."

Tammy paced the waiting room to the lobby as Henry worked on his laptop. The early morning light was just now showing over the horizon of downtown Lexington. Tammy cringed as she saw another news van pulling up to the emergency room parking lot. Someone, and she was guessing Detective Cowell, had called the press and told them a suspect was in custody. Just a half-hour ago, the handsome young detective had strode into the lobby sporting a crisp new suit and a fresh shave.

Tammy was fuming at something else, too. Well, someone else, that is. Jasmine had arrived in full dramatics a couple of minutes ago. Suspiciously, right around the time the news vans first started showing up. She was currently at the nurses' station with her hand on her forehead in a full fit of vapors. Amazingly, she could position herself so that her boobs in the skintight white tank top were fully framed by the glass door where all the media cameras were set up. The display was enough to make Tammy sick. Especially when Detective Cowell made his way over to her. She could just imagine that conversation.

"I can't believe that woman!" Tammy huffed as she took the seat next to Henry.

"Who?" Henry looked up from his laptop for the first time since they arrived and looked around. "Oh." Henry grinned as he enjoyed the Jasmine show.

Tammy smacked his arm. "She's just flaunting herself in front of the media. She doesn't care how Pierce is doing. If she did, then she'd be over here asking about him, not flirting with Detective Cowell."

Henry looked back down at his laptop. "How many news outlets are here?"

"All the local and a couple from Louisville. About six in all. Were you expecting them?"

"Yup. Been working on my statement since we got here. I talked to one of my buddies who practices here in Lexington and he told me Cowell was gunning for a promotion to sergeant. A man with his eye on promotion wouldn't miss the opportunity to be in front of the cameras. I also have some statements prepared for Pierce's family."

Tammy shot to her feet when the door to the exam rooms opened and Pierce came out, handcuffed, with officers on both sides. Tammy had a hard time not racing to him. His eye was completely swollen shut and turning a very nasty dark blue. He had a huge bandage wrapped around his head and looked to be grimacing as the officers pushed him along. Before Tammy had the chance to get to him, Detective Cowell was by his side and forcefully yanking him toward the sea of media lights.

"That will be enough, Detective! If you don't release my client at once, I'll have you before the judge this morning on police brutality charges. And I don't think that will play too well in front of the media," Henry threatened. He stood tall and aggressively marched over to the officers. It was enough to scare the officers back as Henry took one of Pierce's arms and nodded for Tammy to take the other.

"We'll take it from here, gentlemen. Just clear a path, please," Tammy said in her most polite, yet authoritative voice.

"Oh, Pierce!" Jasmine hurled herself onto Pierce the second he came within sight of the news crews with their cameras pressed against the glass. "I was so worried about you!" A well-placed tear trickled down her cheek as she dramatically looked toward the cameras.

"Thanks, Jasmine, but you're hurting me. I have some injuries to my ribs and stomach, so I'd appreciate it if you let go of me." Pierce said through shallow breaths.

Jasmine narrowed her eyes and looked from him to Detective Cowell and out to the media. "This nice young detective told me you murdered someone. Of course, I'm fully cooperating with the investigation." With one last glance showing that Pierce was no longer up to snuff, she flounced her way over to Detective Cowell who put a protective arm around a softly crying Jasmine.

"Don't worry about her, Pierce," Henry whispered. "Focus on getting to that cop car. Keep your head high, but don't smile. You want to look sure of your innocence, but also respectful of the fact Dr. Oldham lost his life."

Pierce just nodded and Tammy felt her heart break for him. She slipped her hand into the crook of his arm and gave him a reassuring smile. "Okay, let's do this."

The officers pushed open the door and they walked out of the hospital and into the bright lights of the cameras. Microphones were shoved in their faces, questions were shouted, and between all of that noise, Tammy could hear the tiny sniffles coming from Jasmine a little way behind them. Oh, what Tammy wouldn't give to plant her fist right in the middle of Jasmine's perfect face.

"Mr. Davies, why did you kill your professor?"

"Was it self-defense?"

"Mr. Davies, are you afraid you'll get the death penalty?"

The reporters shot questions at them faster than bullets. Tammy was being shoved in every direction as reporters tried to get microphones and cameras in Pierce's face. She turned her body inward and shielded Pierce from the media attack with her back. Contrarily, Detective Cowell wouldn't shut up behind them.

Finally they reached the prisoner transport. She felt as if she had fought a battle, but at least he was safe.

"Thank you, Tammy, Henry," Pierce said from the back of the cruiser.

"You're welcome," Tammy almost cried. Pierce sounded so defeated, so broken.

"I'm going with you." Henry slid into the car next to Pierce. "I'll see you processed into jail and then head back to the office to work on your case. We'll talk more about it in the car. Tammy, I've emailed you my notes. Will you please go fill Mr. and Mrs. Davies in on the situation."

"Tammy, could you tell my family I'm sorry. Just, just take care of them for me, okay?" Pierce turned his head away from her and looked out the window as the door was closed before Tammy could respond.

"Without a doubt in my mind, Mr. Davies is guilty and I'll be happily proving that after his arraignment." Tammy turned and saw Detective Cowell standing in front of the news cameras with a sure and slightly cocky look on his face.

"We'll see about that," Tammy murmured under her breath as she made her way to the car. If there were anything she could do to prove that Pierce was innocent, then she'd do it.

Before Tammy stopped her car in front of the large white farmhouse, the door was flung open and Mrs. Davies hurried out onto the veranda and down the stairs. The entire population of the house was outside by the time Tammy opened the car door. She had never felt so many eyes on her at once.

"Tammy, how's my boy? Marshall said I should stay here and let Henry handle the hospital and then I saw the news and they're calling him a murderer! My baby, a murderer!" Mrs. Davies tried to stop the tears from streaming down her face.

The look in her eyes caused Tammy to take a big gulp. She had to tell them, all of them, that the evidence wasn't in his favor and she wasn't quite sure how to do that.

Mr. Davies walked down the steps and put his arm around his wife. "Come inside and tell us what you know and tell us what we can do. There has to be something we can do," Mr. Davies pleaded. His normally tall, strong frame was bent and defeated. He suddenly looked older and with a gentle hand turned his wife toward the house.

Tammy walked up the stairs behind them and nodded as she passed what had to be the whole town. All of the Davieses' friends were in the living room, and, of course, Miss Lily and John Wolfe jockeyed for the first pieces of information as to how Pierce was doing. Tammy gulped and Mrs. Davies took her hand and led her to the living room.

"Please, just tell us what's going on. We're all listening." At Mrs. Davies's soft tone, the room quieted and leaned toward Tammy.

"Well, he has a bruised rib and other bruises on his abdomen. His eye is swollen shut, but luckily the eye and eye socket aren't broken. The worst part is he has an injury to the back of his head that is causing memory loss." The group gasped and whispers started.

"Memory loss?" Mr. Davies asked.

"That's right. He doesn't remember anything about what happened. He remembers the wedding, but nothing until the police busted into his house. Dr. Francis," Tammy nodded her thanks to Deputy Noodle who was standing in the back of the room, "thinks there's a chance his memories will come back as the swelling goes down."

"Oh Lordy," Miss Lily Rose gasped as her hand toyed with the lace collar on her flower print dress. "I know Pierce couldn't have done such a thing, but all this evidence against him! What are we to do?"

"DNA evidence will be back in around ten days. Until then, I don't know. It's so hard to even know where to start when he doesn't remember. Henry is working on the case now. The arraignment will be Monday morning, and the prosecutor from Lexington will surely make a third-party motion asking Judge Cooper to move the case to Lexington given Kenna's relationship with the Davies family. Then there's the media. We need someone from the Davies family, or close to it, to be the spokesperson."

Kenna cleared her throat and stepped forward. "I can't help with the spokesperson part, but I can call the prosecutor and see if we can work something out. I'll let you know what we can agree on," Kenna said as she pulled out her cell phone and walked outside.

"I know I'm new to the family..." Morgan paused and then shrugged, "*very* new. But I have a lot of experience with word-play during negotiations and if you think about it, it's just a word game with the media. One big negotiation with them trying to make you say more than you want."

"I think that's a great idea, honey." Miles wrapped his arm around his new wife and Tammy couldn't help but smile at his show of support.

"Thanks, Morgan. I think you all will want to come up with a short statement to release to the media when you think it's time. Also, Henry wanted you to come up with some standard, short, one- to two-sentence responses for when the media calls or shows up looking for a quote." Tammy looked out the window and saw the sun streaming in. She'd better get to the office and see what she could do to help Henry.

The room was now full of voices as Marcy, the sweet and gentle mother of the Davies kids, moved with the family to the dining room to talk about how to handle the media. Her husband, Jake, wrapped his arm around her in a gesture of complete support. Tammy envied the relationship they shared. Six children and two grandchildren later, Jake still treated Marcy with such love and tenderness of newlyweds.

Miss Lily and John Wolfe were arguing over the gossip they had heard. Ever since the kiss heard round Keeneston, they had been at each other constantly, each trying to outdo the other and be the first to get the scoop in an epic battle of gossips. Miss Lily's white head and John's portly stature were locked in battle against the far wall. No one knew how John got the scoop on just about anything going on in town. Some say it was wiretaps, but Tammy guessed it was aliens. Miss Lily Rae Rose ran the bed and breakfast in town and spent most of her time with her sisters, Daisy Mae and Violet Fae Rose. That's how she got her gossip. Miss Daisy's and Miss Violet's Blossom Café was the heart of the town.

Tammy felt the exhaustion hit her as the adrenaline of the night started to wear off. She gathered her things and said her good-byes. It didn't take long for her to arrive at the law office on Main Street. As she unlocked the door, she looked through the big window and into the lobby. The lights were still off, but it seemed as if she was coming home. She'd been working here since she was seventeen. Nine years. She couldn't believe it.

It took that long just to get Henry to agree to some more feminine touches in the place. She had tried for years, but after

Kenna and Dani started sharing office space, she had the power necessary to push, force, and just not tell Henry of the changes they wanted to make. The main thing being that they got rid of some of the old pictures and put up artwork by local artists along with some lighter-colored furniture and real plants that softened the place. She could see the light coming from Henry's office when she walked into the lobby.

"Tammy? Is that you?" Henry called from behind his desk.

"Yes. Is there any news?" she asked as she hurried into his office.

"Nothing yet. I just need to go meet with Pierce to discuss his arraignment and bond hearing tomorrow. I was wondering if you wanted to come with me?" Henry asked as he stuffed a bunch of papers into his briefcase.

"Yes. I will. He must be so worried. Do you think he'll be able to post bail tomorrow?" Tammy thought to the three hundred and some dollars she had in her savings account and wondered if she should withdraw it in case he needed it.

"I think he will. But, we have to fight over the venue and prosecutor. I'm filing a motion for a special prosecutor to be appointed from out of town. Kenna called and said that she was planning on doing the same. But, I need to prepare him for both options. Ready?"

"Let's go." Tammy walked out the back door and over to Henry's car. If only she knew what to say to make it better.

CHAPTER FOUR

Pierce sat at the table in the jail's common room and watched the morning news. His jaw tightened as Jasmine tearfully accepted the tissue from a local reporter. She dabbed her eyes and took a shuddering breath before saying how horrible she felt for the family of Dr. Oldham. She had no idea her boyfriend could be so cruel.

Pierce leaned back in his seat and crossed his arms across his chest. What could he say? Nothing. He was locked in jail as this woman, for lack of a better word, told the reporter that they were no longer dating. She could never date a murderer. The reporter gave Jasmine's shoulder a supportive squeeze and then sent the camera to another reporter sitting in Dr. Oldham's living room.

Pierce leaned forward in the hard plastic chair as the camera zoomed in on the tired face of Mrs. Oldham. She had bags under her eyes and tears slowly trickled down her slightly wrinkled cheeks. Her salt-and-pepper hair was styled in a short pixie cut that didn't allow any emotion to be hidden as she told the reporter how wonderful her husband was and that she "hoped Pierce Davies gets what he deserves."

Sitting next to Mrs. Oldham was Dr. Oldham's teaching assistant, Aiden Fink. Aiden was the T.A. during the last year of Pierce's master's program. He was a good enough guy who was working toward his Ph.D. Pierce knew that Aiden and the Oldhams spent a lot of time together since Aiden's family was all in Utah. He was a big-time skier. The round glasses and bow tie hid that fact, though.

Aiden nodded. His thinning hair fell to cover his eyes as he grimaced at the reporter's question about Pierce and Dr. Oldham's relationship. Aiden told of Pierce's good grades and that Dr. Oldham and Pierce often worked together late into the night.

A sinking feeling settled in the bottom of his stomach. His mentor's wife, someone he had had countless dinners with, thought he could murder his own friend. Aiden was noncommittal on his answer but was definitely not supporting him either. It was bad enough Jasmine thought it, but it was clear she was just in for the attention. The sinking feeling plummeted ever more. He was going to spend the rest of his life in jail.

"Davies! Your attorney is here." The guard escorted Pierce into the meeting room and locked the door behind him.

"Henry! Tammy! I'm so glad to see you two. How are my parents?" Pierce worried as he took a seat at the metal table.

"They're fine. Your parents love you very much. And Morgan is going to handle the media for them," Tammy told him as she took a seat next to Henry.

Pierce tried to pay attention as Henry explained how the arraignment and bail hearing worked. His eyes kept drifting toward Tammy as she took notes and tried to look reassuring. All Pierce could see were Mrs. Oldham's tears. Had he caused that?

"Pierce." Henry interrupted Pierce's downward thoughts. "You don't say a word to anyone tomorrow unless the judge asks you a direct question. Most likely, Judge Cooper won't speak directly to you. He'll address each question to me. We'll plead not guilty and move for bail to be set immediately due to your roots in the community and the fact you have no priors. Then we'll see if we can raise the money necessary to get you out of jail. Hopefully, by tomorrow afternoon you'll be home."

"Really?" Pierce sat up in his chair, suddenly feeling a little better.

"Yes, really. Just keep your head down, keep quiet, and we'll pull through this," Henry said as he stood up. He looked at Pierce and then at Tammy still sitting in the chair. "Tammy, why don't you stay here while I get the car pulled around and answer any questions Pierce has about his family."

Tammy nodded and then looked over to Pierce. He sat, watching her until Henry left the room.

"Tammy, why are you doing this?" Pierce asked softly. "God knows I don't deserve it for the way I've treated you."

"Pierce, you're a guy. If you were perfect all the time, then you'd be a woman," Tammy teased. She stood up and walked around the table and sat down next to him. "Seriously, right now I'm just worried about you. Is there anything I can do to help you?"

"No, you've done so much." He looked into her face and the worry he was feeling for himself abated. There were dark circles under her eyes. Her naturally light complexion was ghostly after her long night. "Have you slept yet?"

"Not since the night before the wedding. I was just falling asleep when Marshall called me," she told him, the exhaustion clear for all to see.

Pierce stood up and couldn't resist pulling her toward him. She was so small and tired. He felt the immediate urge to protect his little fighter. Her head fit perfectly against his chest as he felt her give a sigh and relax into him. "Go home and get some rest. I need you in that courtroom tomorrow," he spoke into her slightly disheveled blonde hair.

Tammy pulled away and gave him her best shot of a smile. "Don't worry, I'll be there for you." She grabbed her bag and knocked on the door. As she walked, out he thought he heard her say *always*, but it was so soft, he was afraid he imagined it.

Tammy closed her eyes the second Henry started driving. The ride back to Keeneston was way too short. Before she knew it, she was awakened by a curse. She opened her eyes and saw that Marshall had pulled up alongside Henry's car.

"You need to hurry out to Pierce's house. The detectives are out there with our new police dog and handler conducting a search of the property," Tammy heard Marshall say before eliciting another curse from Henry.

"Dammit! What are they after now?" Henry said through gritted teeth as he turned his car to follow Marshall out to Pierce's farm.

"It must be drugs, right?" Tammy remembered the time she met Marko, the police dog Cy had gifted to the Keeneston Police Department at the Christmas party.

"No, the dog is dual-trained, so it could be drugs or explosives. But, probably drugs; pot is my guess." Henry put his foot on the pedal and hurried to catch up to the sheriff's cruiser.

The detectives, a forensic team, and a K-9 vehicle were parked out front when they arrived at the farm. Noodle and Dinky, both Keeneston sheriff's deputies, were keeping a watchful eye on everyone.

Marshall was talking to a tall woman with strawberry blonde hair. A slight dusting of freckles played across her nose and cheeks. She stood in stark contrast to the dark and brooding man sitting next to her in the car. Well, she thought, this should be fun. The athletically built woman looked sweet as sugar and Henry looked like he wanted to light into someone.

Tammy opened the door and walked over to where Marshall stood with the trainer. Her brown dog was resting his black face on his paws as he waited to be put to work.

"Henry Rooney, Tammy Fields, this is Bridget Springer," Marshall introduced.

"Hi, it's nice to meet you both." The polite, slightly Southern voice with a hint of authority made Tammy smile. Something about her made her realize this woman wouldn't be intimidated by anything.

"And what do you think you're doing here now? I mean, don't get me wrong, honey, you're nice to look at, but where are the big boys? I don't want some amateur mucking up a search like this." Henry put his hands on his hips and stared her down.

Tammy almost broke out laughing when Bridget simply smiled sweetly. "I know you've had a long day, Mr. Rooney. I'll make this as painless as possible for you all. Marko is to sweep the area for drugs. The detectives over there seem to think Pierce was dealing." She paused and took her time to slowly look Henry over. "And as for the big boys. Well, I train the big boys, Mr. Rooney. You just try to keep up."

Marshall snorted as Bridget turned with a toss of her hair and headed with Marko over to the house.

"What are you laughing at?" Henry asked Marshall who was grinning ear-to-ear.

"You'd be laughing too with how stupid you just looked. Big boys, huh? Bridget was just explaining the reason it took Marko and her so long to arrive. After Christmas, they were called overseas to train a group of handlers in Afghanistan for the military. Then the president called her and asked a personal favor of her and Marko, which, of course, she couldn't turn down."

"What was it?" Tammy couldn't help but ask. She was too intrigued.

"Bridget was in charge of personal security for the Duchess of Cambridge's baby shower. They had need for a woman who could dress up and blend into the crowd. She acted as the Duchess's assistant and was by her side as her personal bodyguard. That is, after she and Marko swept the area for explosives." Marshall rocked back on his heels and watched Henry's reaction.

Henry looked back at her and then shrugged. "Either way she's pissing me off by looking for drugs. She's messing with my case and my client."

"You don't think I know that? I know what those detectives are doing. If they find drugs, they'll use it as a reason to prevent bail tomorrow," Marshall responded. "But that's not Bridget's fault. I have to cooperate or they'll just say the Keeneston Sheriff Department is covering up evidence on behalf of the sheriff's brother. Yet it's still funny. This may be the first time you messed up with a woman and a pick-up line wasn't involved."

"Well, let's just hope they don't find anything," Henry mumbled as he shoved his hands into his pockets.

"We're about to find out." Tammy watched as Bridget and Marko stepped up to the front door of the house.

Tammy watched as Henry stalked toward Bridget and Marko. They were going to trail her to observe Marko in action. The detectives met them with grudges in the living room. They all stood in the center of the room as not to get in Marko's way.

Bridget brought Marko into the room, *"Zit."* Marko immediately sat and waited his next command. "We're going to start on the far end of the house and then work our way into the kitchen and then head upstairs. Marko, *zoek.*"

Bridget led Marko around the back wall and then to the furniture and cabinets. Marko's tail wagged happily as he stuck his nose under the couch. "Good boy! *Zoek.*"

"What the hell is *zoek?*" Henry whispered.

"Marko's from Holland. He's trained in Dutch commands, Mr. Rooney. *Zoek* is Dutch for *search*. Okay, the living room is clean. Let's move into the kitchen."

Tammy leaned against the car and lifted her face toward the warm afternoon sun. She was so exhausted that she was sure she'd fall asleep where she stood. The house, the garage, and the shed were all clear. No signs of drugs. Marko was now off leash and searching the surrounding woods and fields. Henry, Marshall, and Detective Cowell were still trailing behind Bridget while Detective Basher was nearby on his cell.

She overheard enough to know the police chief was putting pressure on them to find something and to make the case a slam-dunk. As if Pierce's fingerprints all over the murder weapon weren't enough, Tammy thought.

"We found something!" Bridget yelled. "Don't run too fast, Detective Basher, it's not drugs."

Tammy saw the slump to the detectives' shoulders and they started the hike across the yard. "You know, Detective, Pierce is a good man and by focusing on ways to make the evidence fit, you're not looking for the person who is actually responsible."

"So you say. You know how many murderers are nice guys? I'll wait for the DNA evidence, thank you," Basher grunted as they pushed through a bush and into a small crop field hidden by the dense brush. "What did you find?"

"A very heavily locked and concealed outbuilding. Marko's not detecting anything but he should get his nose in there just to verify. I need to know the exact wording of the warrant to see if we have permission to unlock it." Bridget pulled out a tennis ball from the pocket of her black cargo pants and threw it for Marko, who happily snagged it out of the air.

"Yes, we have permission to search every standing structure on the property. Stand aside, I'll cut the locks off." Detective Cowell started to push his way forward when Bridget gave a nice yet very assertive smile and held up her hand.

"Don't worry, Detective. I've got it." Bridget pulled out a small lock-picking case and had the three locks open in less than a minute. "So much cleaner that way. Then we don't have to worry about locking it back up, which is hard to do with broken locks."

Tammy tried to peer in as Bridget opened the camouflaged painted door. Bridget and Marko went in and the rest of them crowded the door to see what was so important it needed to be hidden in a camouflaged building with multiple locks hidden in the woods.

"What the hell is that? Is it an explosive?" Cowell grunted in anger as he realized that Marko had completed his sweep and no drugs were found.

"Nope, it's not an explosive," Bridget said as she pulled out the tennis ball from her pocket again. "It looks like a robot."

"If this is what I think it could be, then I can't believe what I'm seeing," Marshall gasped as he walked around it.

"Can you tell us what this thing is, Sheriff?" Detective Basher asked as he followed Marshall around it.

Tammy slid in the door and looked at the contraption. It was shaped like R2D2 from *Star Wars*, but on steroids. It had tank treads along with a spiky cylinder attachment across its back. There were four mechanical arms, two on each side of the drum-shaped body. The top of the drum appeared to be able to swivel and displayed multiple spray heads. To top off the futuristic machine, there was a computer screen on the "belly" and an old-fashioned trailer hitch above the spikes on the back of it.

"Maybe. There's a debate going on in the farming community concerning agricultural robots. Some say that it defeats the purpose of farming—being out there and tilling the land with their own two hands. Others say it's a miracle. They either can't find or can't afford the help of farm hands needed to bring in and maintain the crops." Marshall walked around it again and just shook his head in amazement.

"So, this thing acts like a farm hand?" Detective Basher wondered as he started at it with a look of slight confusion on his face.

"That's right. If this is what I think it is. I just don't know how," Marshall answered.

"Is it worth killing over?" Detective Basher asked.

Everyone in the room froze at the question. Tammy bit her lip; if Marshall was that amazed, then they all knew the answer to that question.

Tammy forced her legs to move across the gravel parking lot behind the Blossom Café. The only thing keeping her going was knowing her bed was only a flight of stairs away.

Never once did she doubt Pierce. But she'd be naïve if she didn't acknowledge the strong case against him. The loud sounds from the dinner crowd at the café drew her attention away from her worrisome thoughts and refocused them instead on the fact that she hadn't eaten all day. However, a whole circus of flying pigs singing "Howdy Doody" wouldn't be enough to get her to face the town right now.

Unfortunately, fate hadn't finished with her yet. Years of trained instincts came into play as the Rose sisters threw open the back door the second Tammy tried to tiptoe past it. It really was uncanny. It was like they could sense gossip.

"Oh! My poor dear! Bless your little heart, you must be exhausted," Miss Violet pulled Tammy into a tight hug as Miss Daisy and Miss Lily fussed about.

"We made you dinner, dear." Miss Daisy pulled out a large tray from somewhere. Tammy wasn't quite sure where it had come from, but her stomach rumbled as she saw the chicken salad on a large buttery croissant with a glass of sweet tea, a side of fruit, and a huge, honking slice of chocolate cake.

"Let's get you upstairs before you drool all over the place." Miss Lily urged her up the stairs and Miss Violet went back to work in the café.

Tammy opened the door and collapsed in a heap on the second-hand couch she had bought when she was eighteen. She was so proud of how it looked now. After her promotion, she had covered the hunter green-checkered couch with a beautiful tan slipcover and two pink ruffled pillows. The cushions enveloped her as she sank into them.

"Here you go. You need to eat to keep your strength up and bring our boy home." Miss Lily placed the tray on her small coffee table.

"What happened today? Are there any new developments?" Miss Daisy asked.

She had been half-asleep the second she had touched the couch and barely knew the Rose sisters were there. Tammy jumped as someone knocked on the door.

"Don't worry about that, dear, they'll go away soon enough," Miss Lily cooed as she urged Tammy to start talking.

"I know you're in there, Lily Rae! Don't think I wouldn't find out!" The deep voice boomed through the door.

"Is that John Wolfe?" Tammy asked as she hoisted herself up from the depth of the couch.

"It's nothing!" Miss Lily waved her hand in the air and smiled innocently. "Just go on, tell us about your day."

"Well, the bail hearing is tomorrow. That's all I can really tell you, except I was so upset with seeing Jasmine on television. I still can't believe she did that." Tammy shook her head.

"You know I don't like to say a bad word about anyone, but bless her heart, she's nothing but an attention wh…"

"Lily Rae! Open this door at once!" John called from behind the door. Tammy looked to Miss Lily who was just rolling her eyes.

"Go on, dear. You were saying?" Miss Daisy pressed.

"Well, then the detectives did a drug search out at the farm." The Rose sisters gasped in disbelief. "They didn't find anything, of course."

"We had heard the police were out there, but drugs? Never." Miss Lily huffed.

"Tammy? Will you be a dear and let an old man inside?" He called in a sweet voice.

"Ohhh! You old billy goat!" Miss Lily finally responded back.

Tammy decided it was time to throw in the towel. She was swaying on her feet and all she wanted was to eat and crawl into bed. "Okay! That's it." Tammy flung the door open. John's portly frame practically fell into her small apartment. "Good evening, Mr. Wolfe. I'm sorry you can't stay longer, but I was just saying good night to Miss Lily and Miss Daisy. I'm so exhausted I can hardly stand upright. Thank you so much for your gentlemanly concern to come all this way to check on me." Tammy patted his arm and was satisfied by the faint blush of embarrassment that colored his cheeks.

"Well, you get some rest tonight. We'll all be there tomorrow to show our support for our boy." Miss Daisy gave her a rough hug with her wiry frame and then headed back downstairs to fill in the eagerly awaiting dinner crowd. John and Miss Lily looked at each other and then the door. Within seconds, they were both downstairs and regaling the story to the town. Tammy shook her head. She closed her door and locked it before sitting down for dinner. Tomorrow was going to be crucial and she needed all the rest she could get before facing it down.

CHAPTER FIVE

Two officers led Pierce from the cruiser into the back waiting room of the Keeneston Courthouse. It felt great just to be back in his hometown. He was seated with various other prisoners and the feeling of relief was quickly replaced with one of dread. What if Judge Cooper was replaced? What if he didn't get bail? What if everyone thought he was guilty? What if he *was* guilty?

The questions assaulted him so much so that he failed to see Dinky come into the room. After hearing his name, Pierce finally looked up and saw Deputy Dinky standing in front of him.

"It's time, buddy."

Pierce nodded his head and took a deep breath. His hands were shaking as he stood up and followed Dinky into the courtroom. A quick look around confirmed what he feared—it was packed. He saw the Rose sisters in the front row next to his family. The sheriff's department was standing off to the side. Jasmine was quietly dabbing tears away as she was ensconced in the middle of the Belles. Mrs. Oldham and Aiden were on the other side of the courtroom staring daggers at him. And Marianne was sitting with her pen and paper at the ready to take notes for the Keeneston paper.

Pierce swallowed hard and locked eyes with Tammy sitting at the defense desk next to Henry. She gave him a reassuring smile and he felt the panic subside slightly. Henry stood and buttoned his suit coat. The shiny contraption was almost enough to make

Pierce laugh, except the man in that tacky ensemble was the one he was depending on to get him out of jail.

Standing at the prosecutor's table was a very political-looking man in the standard black suit and red power tie combination. McKenna was sitting next to him talking to a third man. That third man was rumpled and looked slightly frazzled.

"Take a breath, Pierce. Don't smile, but don't look so petrified. Be confident in your innocence," Henry said as he shook his hand.

They took a seat behind the desk and Pierce tried to look confident. He leaned over to Tammy and whispered, "Who are those men next to Kenna?"

"The pompous peacock is Alexander Griffin III, the Lexington D.A. He's running for mayor and wants this case for the publicity. The other man is Jimmy Hickson. Kenna has asked for him to be appointed as the special prosecutor. He may not look it, but he's brilliant. He also has the reputation as the most fair and incorruptible prosecutor in the commonwealth," Tammy whispered back.

Noodle came into the courtroom from a door behind the bench and called the court to order. Pierce tried to remember to breathe as he rose to stand next to Henry. Judge Cooper looked through the file, but before he could call for the plea, Alexander stood up with his most politically serious face on. He buttoned his black suit coat and cleared his throat, all the while his perfectly swooped hair never dared to move.

"Your Honor, if I may? Alexander Griffin, representing the Lexington D.A.'s office."

"Yes, I know who you are, Mr. Griffin. I've also received your lengthy motion to transfer the case to your jurisdiction," Judge Cooper's gruff voice rang out. Pierce had to hope that slightly annoyed voice boded well for keeping the case in Keeneston.

Kenna stood and smiled in direct contradiction to Alexander. "Your Honor, you'll find my response in the file and I would ask that special prosecutor James Hickson be appointed. This will allow Mr. Davies's arraignment and bail hearing to continue without undue delay to his rights."

"I object!" Alexander puffed up and shot a dagger at Kenna's smiling face.

"Mr. Hickson, I've heard many good things about you. Are you prepared to step into this case immediately?" Judge Cooper asked, ignoring Alexander's interpretation of a fish as he gasped indignantly.

"I am, Your Honor." Jimmy Hickson stood up and tried to smooth the deep wrinkles from his seersucker suit.

"Then, I'm ready to rule. Mr. Griffin, as the crime took place in Keeneston, so should the trial. I am denying your motion to change venue. Ms. Ashton, due to your conflict of interest with the defendant your Motion for Appointment of Special Prosecutor is approved." Judge Cooper signed some papers and then turned to Pierce.

"This is your part. So far it's good for us. Don't say a thing unless directly asked," Henry whispered before turning to Judge Cooper.

"How does your client plead to the charge of first degree murder, Mr. Rooney?"

"Not guilty, Your Honor, and we request bail to be set."

Tammy tried to hold it together as she followed the family home. Pierce was never going to make bail. She heard the audible gasp from his parents when the judge set it at one million dollars. Tears fell down Marcy's face as Jake led her out of the courthouse. Henry had sent Tammy with them to see if there was a way they could pull the cash together for the required ten percent to secure a bond for Pierce's release from jail. She parked the car in the now-full driveway in front of the white farmhouse and headed into the living room where the family was gathering.

Paige placed her son, Ryan, on the floor with Annie and Cade's daughter, Sophie, and then sat quietly on the sofa holding Cole's hand tightly. Tammy felt as if she were intruding on a private moment for the Davies family and tried to hide against the front window as the family began discussing how much money they could get their hands on.

"Marshall, I know you have that money saved up to help Katelyn expand her clinic. You better not offer that until your wife gets here and okays it. I wouldn't feel right otherwise." Marcy's small hand patted Marshall's large one as she sighed and leaned back in her chair. Exhaustion and worry were written all over her face.

Tammy tapped Annie on the shoulder and leaned forward, "Where is Katelyn?" she whispered.

"Said she had a quick errand to run, probably to the clinic. She'll be here soon," Annie replied.

"Thank you all so much, but it's clear we don't have the cash to get Pierce home tonight. Tomorrow we'll see about putting the farm up as collateral with a bail bondsman," Marcy said, choking back tears. Jake pulled her up from the chair and into his arms as she broke down.

Embarrassed to see such an intimate moment, Tammy turned with her own tears heavy behind her eyes and looked out the window. With a gasp her eyes widened and her heart pounded so loudly she didn't hear Annie asking what was the matter. Tammy fought the handle to the door and threw it open just in time for Katelyn and Pierce to walk into the living room.

No one moved. No one said a word. Everyone stared in disbelief as Pierce stood there smiling. Finally Marcy gulped back her tears and ran across the room and enveloped Pierce in a fierce motherly hug.

"How? Katelyn, did you do this?"

"What's the use of a trust fund if you don't use it every once in a while? Besides, we're family," Katelyn said with a smile and a slight shrug.

A soft knock at the door stopped Marcy from suffocating Katelyn in a hug. She opened the door and the Rose sisters filed in with casserole dishes piled high, followed by Kenna, Will, Mo, Dani, and Ahmed hidden behind large carrying cases packed with food.

Kenna and Will had a farm not to far away with Will's parent's, Betsey and William living close by. Tammy had gotten to know Will, a retired NFL Quarterback turned race horse owner, since she started working with Kenna and really liked him as a good country boy. Mo, or more formally Mohtadi Ali Rahmen, was a prince of a small country named Rahmi in the Middle East. Smooth was the only way to describe him. He was as relaxed as you could be in thousand dollar suits. Being the youngest son, he left the country and pursued his passion, horse racing. Now his passions included his wife, Danielle whom everyone called Dani, and their unborn child. If Mo and Dani's child was a boy, he'd be the heir to the small island country due to problems of others in his family were having conceiving a male. Ahmed, Mo and Dani's head of security and all around badass, gave her a wink as he carried the food to the kitchen.

"Don't worry about a thing, Marcy. We got enough food for everyone! We didn't want you worrying about nothing while we work this out." Miss Lily walked past Pierce and shot him a wink as she headed into the kitchen followed by her sisters.

"I hope you all don't mind us dropping by either," Will said as he gave Marcy a peck on the cheek before shaking Pierce's hand.

"Not at all, dear! You all are part of our family. Dani, bless your heart, take a seat and put those feet up. Just three more months to go to meet that little one. How are you two holding up?" Marcy asked as she escorted Dani to the nearest chair.

"I feel great, thank you. I'm a little worried about leaving, though," Dani gave a little smile to Mo, who returned it with one of his own.

"Yes, we leave next month for Rahmi. The baby must be born there in case it is a boy and heir to the kingdom. There are all kinds of ceremonial events and procedures we'll have to go through if Dani provides us with an heir. Luckily, our doctor agreed to fly out around her due date to take care of her. And of course, you all are more than welcome! Dani wants all her family there, which means we need to take care of little brother. How are you doing, Pierce?" Mo asked as he shifted into his no-nonsense business voice.

"I'm exhausted and starving," Pierce said with a little laugh as he finished getting hugs from his brothers.

"I heard that! Give me one second and we'll have lunch ready for everyone!" Miss Violet called from the depths of the kitchen.

Pierce savored every bite of the pecan-encrusted catfish as he listened to his brothers tease their wives and his mother fussing over the babies. It felt almost normal. Almost. The look on Tammy's face when she opened the door said it all. They didn't think he'd ever come home. When Katelyn knocked on the door as he and Henry were discussing the case, he thought he was imagining things. But his sister-in-law strutted into the room and placed a cashier's check for the full bond on the table and told him it was time to go home.

He had asked her on the drive to the farm why she'd give so much of her money to get him out of jail. Katelyn gave him a smile and said she had a feeling that it would be refunded in no time when the charges were dropped. Then she winked and she said she'd then use the money as an investment in Pierce. Pierce gave up wondering what it meant and just enjoyed being out of jail.

"Pierce, do you think you're up to telling us what happened?" Miles asked quietly, but it wasn't quiet enough. All the comforting noises stopped and everyone froze as they waited to hear what he'd say. Did they not think he'd tell them if he could?

"I'm sorry, I just don't remember." Pierce set down his food and waited. He knew it would come.

"Have you tried working backwards? Start with your most recent memories and go back?" Paige asked.

"I don't remember. I'm sorry." Pierce took a breath and hoped it would be the end of it.

"It's in there somewhere, you just have to find a way to get it out," Cade said as he took a bite of his sandwich.

"Don't you think I know that?" Pierce tossed down the napkin and slid his chair back. "But that doesn't help me. Nothing has helped me remember. And why don't you discuss with Kenna the consequences in court if I can't put forth any argument except 'I don't remember.'"

Pierce knew his family was simply trying to understand what happened, but it was just too much. He couldn't have them all staring at him as if the memories would come back at any second. "Excuse me for a moment, please." Pierce stood up and avoided looking at his family before ducking out the front door.

He closed his eyes and took a deep breath. He wanted to feel the breeze and listen to the world. Instead he heard a car door close and heels tapping along the walkway. Opening his eyes, Pierce didn't even try to hide the curse as Jasmine approached him a denim miniskirt and white blouse.

"What the hell are you doing here?" Pierce growled as he put his hands on his hips and moved to the top of the porch stairs.

"That's a nice way to welcome your girlfriend," Jasmine tried to tease as she smiled up at him from the bottom of the stairs.

"So, not only are you good at throwing me under the bus to the cameras, you're also delusional."

"I'm sorry, Pierce. I always believed in you. I was just so scared of what was going to happen to you and the media just pushed those cameras into my face. I didn't even know what was happening! That's why I came here. I want you to know that I will be by you, my boyfriend, every step of the way showing you how much I love you." Jasmine tried to look reassuring as she put one heeled foot on the bottom stair and gave a little pout of her lower lip.

"Let's get one thing clear. You are not my girlfriend. Our relationship ended the second you stepped in front of the cameras and started bad-mouthing me." Pierce held up his hand as Jasmine opened her mouth to argue. "And as for standing by my side, you wouldn't even know how to do that. The only woman doing that so far is Tammy. You weren't by my side as I was arrested. You weren't by my side when I was at the hospital or when I was being hauled into the police car on television. You weren't even by my side this morning in court!" Pierce couldn't believe Jasmine would even show up here. That pout, which before this weekend he loved, only infuriated him now.

"Tammy? You're comparing me to Tammy? Now that's a laugh. I'm a woman, she's just a kid in a boy's body. Maybe it's true what they say about what goes on in jails if you're trying to compare a woman like me to that…flat-chested, short, boy-cut girl." Jasmine crossed her arms and pushed up her ample chest and let her nails come out as she realized Pierce wasn't going to welcome her back with open arms.

Pierce strode down the stairs and stopped right above her. "Get out of here before I call Marshall out here to arrest you for trespassing." Jasmine narrowed her eyes and tossed her long hair over her shoulder as she turned to walk away.

"Oh, and Jas," Pierce called out as he waited for her to turn back around.

"What?"

"You'll never be half the woman Tammy is."

Tammy stood rooted in place at the door. She had snuck out of the dining room to check on Pierce, only to have opened the door in time to hear Jasmine ripping her to shreds. Tammy had finally been pushed to the limits. She wasn't a confrontational person at all. She much preferred to laugh, tease, and be happy. She tended to avoid the more unpleasant parts of life. She figured growing up in the mobile home with a father who drank himself to death was enough unpleasantness to deal with. But, hearing Jasmine set her off.

She had taken just one step onto the porch when Pierce had called out to Jasmine. Tammy froze when she heard the most beautiful words she had ever heard come out of his mouth. He thought she was more of a woman than Jasmine. He had never seen her as a woman before and not only that, but to defend her. Tammy felt the electricity of excitement run through her body. Could it be true, after two years of doing everything she could to get his attention, that Pierce finally saw her for who she was?

Pierce turned and his eyes widened slightly as he saw her standing there. Tammy couldn't help the smile that came over her face. "Thank you for sticking up for me, Pierce."

"It was nothing," Pierce mumbled as he walked up the stairs.

Tammy reached out and placed her hand on his arm. She felt the muscles bunch beneath her touch. "It was something to me. No one has ever stood up for me before."

"Don't do this, Tammy," Pierced warned.

"Do what?" Tammy asked, confused.

"This. What you want, what you've wanted for two years." Pierce waved his hands about in agitation and Tammy's hope plummeted. "After all you've done for me over the past couple of days, I have come to realize something. I was stupid and blind. You're a wonderful woman. More than I deserve."

"Pierce…" Tammy started to say, but he cut her off.

"I just need to get out of here. Please tell everyone thank you. I just need some time to myself right now." Pierce bounded down the stairs and hopped into his farm truck he had left at his parents' house the night of Miles and Morgan's wedding. Tammy stared after him. What had just happened? She didn't know for sure, but it sure felt as if her heart had just been broken.

Pierce sat in the beat-up truck and looked out the windshield at his house. Crime tape was hanging from the door, his grass was trampled, and he sat worrying about what he'd find when he got inside. The memory of waking up to Dr. Oldham's body was all he could think about. The vision just wouldn't leave him.

Pierce got out of the truck and looked around the farm. He worried about the secret he and Dr. Oldham kept. Heading off into the woods, Pierce decided to make sure it hadn't been discovered yet before going into his house again.

He pushed through the shrubs and into the clearing. The camouflaged storage unit was still locked and Pierce sighed in relief. He unlocked the door and stood staring at his invention. Satisfied everything was all right, he locked the door back up and headed home. It was time to face whatever demons were inside.

Pierce made the walk back to his house thinking of his close partnership with Dr. Oldham. He had been more than just a mentor. He had been a friend. Pierce stopped at his front door and slowly pushed it open. All evidence of the murder was gone. The carpet where Dr. Oldham had laid was removed, collected as evidence against Pierce. He looked around at the destruction.

Fingerprint powder was everywhere. Drawers were emptied, his things tossed about the entire house. "Aw, welcome home. Feed me!" Gus squawked from his cage in the living room.

"How you doing, Gus?" Pierce asked as he opened the cage door. Gus jumped out and climbed up Pierce's arm.

"Aw, Gus is a good bird." Gus nuzzled his beak against Pierce's ear and rode on his shoulder into the kitchen.

Pierce sat Gus down on the kitchen table with a banana as he started the long process of cleaning up his house. As he scrubbed the fingerprint dust from the doorframe, he cursed himself for the way he had treated Tammy—today, yesterday, hell, for the past two years.

When he was in high school, he looked nothing like he did now. Pierce cringed as he remembered how he was all sharp knees and elbows. He was tall, gangly, and had braces. He disappeared into their shadows when he stood next to his brothers. Miles, Marshall, and Cade had all developed early. They played sports, had muscles and girlfriends. He and Cy had taken a little longer to develop. But even Cy had turned into a man sooner than Pierce. Back then, the only reason girls talked to him was to get info on his brothers.

Tammy had been nice, though. She had smiled when they passed each other in the hall and she had never talked to him solely to get the scoop on the other Davies brothers. In fact, she hadn't ever really talked to anyone. She hadn't been part of the "in crowd" either. The Belles had made sure no one got to know Trailer Park Tammy. Yes, she held her head high and smiled at everyone, but she was never part of the class.

When Pierce went off to college, he grew three more inches and gained almost forty pounds of muscle. His facial hair filled in and he started wearing short stubble just because he could. Girls started noticing him, too. Now it was his roommate who was hounded by girls wanting to know what Pierce liked. Needless to say, college made up for high school.

Though he still worked his parents' farm, he spent most of his time in Lexington on campus. He chose to hang at the campus bars instead of the Blossom Café. Then a little over two years ago, he had run into Tammy again. She hadn't changed one bit.

She was cute, bubbly, and still very nice, although a bit more forward than she had been in the past. But when she hit on him, it only stroked his ego. He never bothered to actually look past the fact that she still looked like she was sixteen. She didn't have the womanly curves he had grown used to on others. And so he had been shallow and ignored her.

His indifference toward Tammy lasted until Christmas this past year. That was when Cy had pulled her into a kiss. She had thrown her arms around him and kissed him with such wild abandoned passion that he was instantly enamored. When Cy caressed her bottom, Pierce realized she had a perfectly shaped one. Then he noticed the way her breasts pushed against Cy's chest and noticed that while they were small, they were perky and he was itching to feel them. However, it hadn't been enough to draw him away from his plaything.

Now when he was at the lowest point of his life, Tammy had been there. She wasn't hitting on him, she was supporting him. Even more than his so-called girlfriend had done and he realized just how *dumb* he had been. Why did it take such a tragedy to open his eyes only to show him something he couldn't have? There was no way he was going to get involved with her now as he stood trial for murder. He couldn't do that to her or her reputation.

Tammy kicked off her shoes and poured herself a glass of wine. She had stayed at the Davies farm for a short while after Pierce left and fielded questions from his family. Then she made her way to the office and spent the afternoon and most of the evening going through case law for Pierce's lack-of-memory defense. Finally she had thrown in the towel and headed home.

A strong knock at the door had her hurrying to open it. She was woman enough to admit she hoped it was Pierce coming to kiss her and confess his undying love for her. Cliché, yes… but it didn't mean she wasn't thinking it.

"I knew you'd come by," she said with a smile as she opened the door. Years of maintaining a sunny personality even when she didn't feel like it kept the smile in place.

"You did? Impressive, considering I didn't even know until a little while ago when I called you for the fifth time and finally gave up. I decided to come here instead." Demetri's Greek voice purred with a hint of aggravation.

"Oh, I'm sorry, Demetri. It's just this case I'm on. My time has not been my own these past couple of days." Tammy opened the door to her apartment and watched as he strutted in.

"Your client—it's the guy you told me about, isn't it? The one who ignored you all those years?" Demetri asked as he poured a second glass of wine.

"Yes, it's Pierce. Look, Demetri, we need to talk." Tammy took a sip of her wine and looked up as Demetri set down his glass.

"I figured that when I didn't hear from you for two days. It was easy enough to figure out that you're still not over him, are you?"

"No, I'm not," Tammy confessed.

Demetri set his glass down and looked at her with a mix of anger and pity. "He'll never love you, you know?"

Tammy shrugged her shoulders in answer. "I'm willing to take that chance."

CHAPTER SIX

Tammy rolled over onto her back and stared at the ceiling. Demetri was pissed, but was he right? Did she have no chance with Pierce? She slapped her hands on the mattress and pushed herself up. She might not have a chance with him, but Tammy could find out what happened to him.

She jumped out of bed and slid into a royal blue flowing skirt, slipped on a pale pink tank top, slid her feet into worn brown cowboy boots, and grabbed her purse. It was a little after eleven at night—a perfect time to hit the bars!

As Tammy drove to Lexington, she remembered that Pierce's truck was still at the wedding reception after he left. Lexington, even being called the "big city," was anything but. It only had two cab companies and only one of those would come to surrounding towns.

Tammy pulled out her cell phone and called Zippy Cab's dispatch. "Yeah, where can Zippy take you?" The operator barked into the phone as she smacked on what sounded like bubble gum.

"Hi. I was hoping you could help me. On Saturday my boyfriend was picked up from a wedding in Keeneston. He had gotten a little deep into his cups and kinda took off with our wedding gift," Tammy said sheepishly.

"Uh-huh." The dispatch operator sounded disbelieving so Tammy figured she needed to make the story complete.

"His damn brother brought pure grain hooch... to a wedding! Who does that? After a couple drinks, my man thought he could do anything. Apparently while I was in the bathroom, he stole a couple presents and hopped in the cab! Anyway, he ended up at home but with such a hangover he didn't even talk to me for the rest of the day. When I asked where the gravy boat was that we got the bride and groom, he didn't remember. The whole evening was gone! So I'm trying to track down that gravy boat. It cost me forty-five dollars!" Tammy said outraged.

"Oh, hon, I understand. I got me one of those, too. Let's see. We only had one pick-up in Keeneston Saturday night. Yup, in the driver's notes, he mentioned he was drunk as a skunk. Dropped him off at Classics," the woman said kindly. "My advice, kick his ass to the curb. No matter how great the sex is, they're never worth the hassle."

"Thank you and I know what you mean." Tammy hung up and headed for Classics. It wouldn't be too busy on a Monday night. Hopefully, the bartender would remember something.

She pulled into the mostly empty parking lot and headed inside. A local band was playing to a group of thirty or so students who were hanging out with beers in their hands. She looked around and found her way to the bar. A hot, young male student was working behind the bar and came up to her the second she sat down.

"What can I do you for?" he asked with a smile, the double entendre not lost on her.

"Hi. Were you working here Saturday?" Tammy asked with a flutter of her lashes.

"Nope, sorry. But I do get off in an hour," he said leaning against the bar.

"Thanks. But not tonight." Tammy slid off the bar stool and felt the disappointment weighing on her shoulders. She stood outside and wondered what to do next when she noticed two frat guys stumbling away from Classics and walking further into downtown. *Is this what Pierce did?*

Tammy started following them and saw them go into a dive bar a block away. She peeked in the door and was assaulted by the stench of drunk men watching telecast horse racing on old televisions. Across the street, men in suits and women in dresses sat in front of the large glass windows as a man played a piano. Tammy looked back and forth between the two bars and only took a second to realize which one a drunk Pierce would have walked into.

Tammy took a deep breath and sauntered into the dive bar. She moved to the bar and ignored the look of the men on either side of her. Tammy sent the old bartender a smile and pulled out her cell phone.

"What'll ya have, ma'am?" the gruff bartender asked.

"Actually, I was hoping you'd help me. Did you work Saturday night?" Tammy held her breath as she waited for him to answer.

"Yup. I own this place. I'm here every night but Sunday."

Tammy opened the picture of Pierce on her phone. She wasn't going to tell anyone why she had it, or the fact that she might have taken it a year ago when he wasn't looking. "Was this man in here that night? It would have been sometime around midnight."

"Let me see." The man took the phone and looked at it for a moment before handing it back. "Yup. He was drunker than a fiddler on the roof, that one was."

"Thank you. Did he leave here with anyone? Or catch a cab home?"

The bartender cocked his head and looked her over. He wasn't going to answer. "I know who you are. You're the pretty lady attorney for that boy standing trial for murder. I gotta say I'm surprised the police haven't been snooping around."

"Would you mind telling me what you remember about Mr. Davies?" Tammy asked with as much honey to her voice as she could muster.

"Sure. He drank two glasses of bourbon, complained about Greece, or something like that, and then tossed down a huge tip and then headed down the street toward the courthouse."

"Thank you so much for your help!" Tammy jumped off the stool with a renewed energy. There were at least five bars between here and the courthouse, and she'd visit them all if it meant helping Pierce.

Tammy headed back down the street and skipped over some yuppie bars until she found another hole-in-the-wall place. She walked into the dark bar and had to wait for her eyes to adjust. A local country band was playing and the place was surprisingly full. Tammy made her way to the bar.

"Excuse me!" She waved to the bartender. When he arrived, she held out her phone with Pierce's picture. "Was this man in here on Saturday night?"

"I don't know. I wasn't working then, but Zack was. He's the server over there." The bartender pointed to a man setting down drinks at one of the many standing tables.

"Thank you!" Tammy called out as she moved to intercept the waiter. "Excuse me!" Tammy waved as the waiter hurried toward the bar.

"Yes?"

"Do you remember this man here on Saturday night around midnight?" Tammy showed him the picture and held her breath.

"Yeah, I do. He was drunker than a hillbilly at a rooster fight. He was complaining about Greece invading our state and stealing our women."

Tammy tried not to laugh, but she was starting to understand the Greek references. "Did he leave here in a cab?"

"Nope. Some people took him home. I was going to call a cab, but they told me they had it."

"Do you remember what they looked like? Their names? Anything?" Tammy asked as she felt her excitement growing.

"Not really. Just remember one of them was a tall, stronger fellow. He ran into me as they were helping your friend outside. Now, if you'll excuse me, I need to get this drink order in."

"Thank you so much for your time." Tammy flashed him a smiled and hurried out of the dark bar. She couldn't wait to tell Pierce what she had found.

Pierce tossed and turned in his bed as he tried to control the thoughts running through his head. They just wouldn't stop. Images of Tammy dancing with her date at Miles's wedding flashed through his head along with memories of shooting bourbon and then waking up to Dr. Oldham's body. No matter what he did, he couldn't escape it. He couldn't shut it off.

Deciding sleep was just not going to happen, Pierce rolled out of bed and tossed on a pair of athletic shorts. He schlepped down the stairs and was turning into the kitchen when he sensed something wasn't right.

Pierce narrowed his eyes and scanned the dark kitchen but didn't see anything. He was just jumping at shadows, surely a result from not sleeping since that horrible night.

Turning back around and heading for the living room, Pierce called out, "Gus, wanna watch some television? I'll even try to find your favorite show…"

Before Pierce could finish his sentence, the shadow in front of him moved. Prongs shot out and connected to his chest. His muscles spasmed as he lost control of his legs and collapsed to the ground. Peirce groaned as he felt hands grabbing him under the arms and start dragging him across the floor.

He tried to kick out, but his legs wouldn't respond. Panic welled as the dark figure hauled his unresponsive body onto a living room chair. Ropes tightened around him as he strained to see who was tying him up. The man was strong and of average height but completely covered in black. Pierce willed himself to struggle as the ropes tightened across his chest and dug into arms. The sounds of duct tape being ripped instilled a new level of fear as his feet were taped together and then his hands.

The man's shadow appeared before his face again and for a split second Pierce saw the whites of his teeth in the darkness as the man smiled. "Goodbye, Mr. Davies." The man's voice triggered something in the back of Pierce's mind. It was familiar somehow, but before he could remember, the taser was pressed to his bare chest once again and Pierce slowly faded into the night.

Tammy turned onto the small country road leading to Pierce's farm and pressed on the gas. This late at night there wouldn't be anyone on the roads. Her headlights outlined the black four-board fences as she passed pastures full of cows, horses, and crops that sparkled in the moonlight.

She'd have enjoyed the drive more if she weren't so afraid of what Pierce would think when she turned up at his house. "I wonder if he sleeps naked?" Tammy asked herself with a grin.

Tammy cruised around the sweeping curve in the road and gasped as a pair of headlights came right at her. Slamming on her brakes and swerving off the road, Tammy managed to avoid the accident. She cursed as she caught a glimpse of a larger man driving and a smaller figure in the passage seat.

"Asshole!" Tammy yelled out her window at the rapidly disappearing car. She got out of her car and walked around it, making sure there was no damage before pulling out of the grass and back onto the road.

Tammy kept her window down and let the wind blow her short hair around her face. Before long the incident with the other driver was out of her mind. Much to her chagrin, she was completely wrapped up imagining knocking on the door to Pierce's house. Pierce answered wearing nothing but a towel slung low around his hips, having just emerged from a shower. Okay, it was almost guaranteed he wouldn't be taking a shower at two-thirty in the morning, but this was her fantasy and he was wet and naked in it.

He'd open the door and smile down at her. Pierce would run his hand slowly down her arm and take her hand into his, pulling her close. His wet body would dampen her shirt, exposing the fact that she wasn't wearing a bra underneath it. With a wicked smile, Pierce would notice and flames would flicker... no, wait! Flames really were flickering across the dark skyline.

Smoke danced in the moonlight as Tammy pressed hard on the gas pedal and dialed 9-1-1. She knew instantly where the fire had originated. She just hoped Pierce was burning brush and it wasn't what she feared.

As Tammy drove closer, she knew her prayers weren't answered. Smoke was pouring out of Pierce's house. The back of the house where she remembered the kitchen to be was engulfed in flames.

Tammy leapt from her car and ran to the front door. As she opened the door, smoke assaulted her and pushed her back. She coughed to inhale fresh air. A figure drew her attention, though. Through the smoke she thought she saw Pierce sitting in a chair. Pulling up her shirt to cover her mouth, Tammy took a deep breath and rushed in, keeping as low as she could.

"Tammy?" Pierce coughed.

"Get up, hurry!" Tammy called as she rushed toward him.

"I can't. I'm tied up. Get out. Save yourself." Pierce yelled, his voice husky from the smoke.

"Aw, save Gus! Save Gus! That's a good bird," Gus squawked from the bottom of his cage.

Tammy hurried to the cage and opened the door. Gus jumped out and climbed up her arm. Reaching into her cowboy boot, she pulled out her knife. With a flip of the wrist, the sharp blade flicked out and Tammy set to work on the rope around Pierce's bare chest. Apparently fate had a sense of humor as she thought of her dream to keep from panicking.

"Where did you get a knife?" Pierce asked in amazement as she pulled off the rope.

"I'm a country girl. Doesn't everyone carry one?" She asked as she slid the blade down the duct tape tied around his ankles.

The crackle of the fire drew Pierce's attention away from her work. "Tammy, I don't want to pressure you, but can you hurry?"

Tammy looked over her shoulder as the flames licked the hall wall. The front door was now engulfed in flames and they were running out of ways to get out. She sliced the tape and went to work on his wrists. In seconds she was able to free him.

Tammy backed away from the fire and looked around the living room. "Can we open the window?" Tammy asked as she rushed to the large plate glass window at the end of the house.

"You bet we can." Pierce rolled Gus's large metal cage across the room and with a shove, it fell into the window. The glass cracked and burst under the force of the cage's impact. "Ladies first."

Pierce held out his hand and Tammy took it. Gus's nails clung to the tiny strap of her shirt and dug into her skin as she climbed on top of the cage and crawled out into the fresh air. In the distance she heard the old wood house crackle as Pierce climbed his way out of the living room. He jumped to the ground and pulled Gus's cage through the window.

"Looks like this may be all I can save. It's a good thing I hadn't moved any of my good stuff into this house yet." Pierce held out his hand and Gus jumped onto it as Pierce put him on his perch. "Tammy, you saved me. I don't know how I can ever thank you."

The house groaned suddenly and Pierce leaped on top of Tammy, forcing her to the ground. The house heaved and the windows exploded from the heat of the fire around them. Lights from the local Keeneston Volunteer Fire Department and the sheriff's department reflected off the grass as they pulled to a stop on the dirt driveway.

Tammy sighed. After all these years of throwing herself at Pierce, he finally jumped her. And he was half-naked! She felt his bare legs against hers and his solid chest was pressed tight against her back as he cradled her head in his arms. Too bad Marshall's booted feet came into view as cops and firefighters surrounded them.

"Pierce! Tammy! Are you okay?" Marshall asked as he skidded to a stop next to Tammy's head and helped Pierce up.

"Yeah, I'm okay. Thanks to Tammy." Pierce held out his hand and helped Tammy from the ground.

Annie rushed over with some water and towels. "Yes, thank goodness she was driving by, saw the smoke, and called 9-1-1. Here, to wash your face and drink." Annie handed Tammy the water and towel.

"She didn't just place the call. She saved my life!" Pierce told them as he poured a bottle of water on his face, the ash and soot running down his bare chest and sliding over his abs. Tammy stared and ran her tongue over her lower lip. Thank goodness her face was covered in soot or else everyone would see that she was flustered for a whole other reason than the fire.

Noodle and Emma Francis hurried over along with Dinky and Chrystal, Annie's cousin. Apparently, the two couples were getting serious. Dr. Francis took in every inch of them as she stood there, trying to ascertain if they were injured. Chrystal was staying close to Dinky's side as he alternated between pride at having her there and embarrassment because he arrived at Pierce's farm wearing camouflaged pajamas and duck slippers.

Within minutes, the whole herd of Davies family members were there, along with Henry and Ahmed. As always, Henry was somehow dressed in a suit, even though it was now almost four in the morning. Marcy fussed over Pierce, Jake looked on worriedly, Paige hugged her brother tightly, and Katelyn checked on Gus.

"Why don't you start at the beginning," Marshall told him, stepping further away from the house as the fire hoses were turned on the burning structure.

Tammy cleaned up her face as she listened to how Pierce was attacked and tied to the chair before the house was set afire. She blushed as he told them how she had rescued him and then how they had escaped the flames as they started to come into the living room.

"Knife in the boot, nice!" Annie smiled as Tammy dried off her face.

"Yes, I am very proud of you, Tammy. You're a brave woman," Ahmed told her as he took off his ever-present black suit coat and draped it over her shoulders. A rush of pleasure heated her up more than the coat as Pierce looked jealously on.

"What I don't understand is why this is happening to you?" Marcy cried as she kept a tight hold on her youngest son.

"I think I may know why," Henry said as he pulled out a piece of paper from his brief case. "Mrs. Oldham and Aiden Fink just filed a lawsuit claiming rights to the invention you created with Dr. Oldham's help. They are declaring that they are solely responsible for that patent and that you stole it."

"Wait. They're saying the Cropbot is theirs?" Pierce couldn't believe it. How did they even know about it?

"Yes. They appear to have the evidence of it, too." Henry told him as he handed the complaint to Pierce.

"That's impossible. I never gave my notes to anyone. Not even Dr. Oldham. They are secure in a bank vault."

"Is the Cropbot what we found in the shed back there during the drug sweep?" Marshall asked.

"You found it?"

"If it looks like R2D2 on steroids, then yes, we saw it," Tammy told him.

Miles interrupted by holding up his hand. "I'm beginning to think you've been keeping secrets. What is this all about?"

"The Cropbot is an invention I created during my last year of the master's program. I had been studying crop growth and soil composition when I discovered that I could grow more crops and bigger crops if the fields were better maintained. For example, in a small quarter-acre garden that could be tended in full everyday, the soil was better quality than a ten-acre plot that was only just watered after being planted."

Pierce continued. "So, I developed the Cropbot. It's an automated farm hand and can travel the length of your field and till the land, keeping weeds out naturally by keeping the soil fresh, watered, and aerated between crops. Further, I attached different spray heads so the Cropbot can spray organic pesticides as it rolls by." Pierce watched his family as they looked at him in disbelief.

"How does it operate?" Miles asked with both curiosity and disbelief showing on his face.

"By cell phone. There's a computer in it that takes soil samples in different areas of the fields so I know if it needs fertilizing. I created an app for it. I just pull it up and pull up the GPS and touch the field I want it to go to and select the functions I want it to perform. Off it goes. I have been testing it for two years and every year my crops are more abundant and of better quality than the year before. The field keeps getting better as opposed to worn. No more questions on how much to water or how much to fertilize. The Cropbot computes all of it based on the soil tests," Pierce explained.

"This is amazing, Pierce. I don't know what to say." Miles shook his head and then pulled Pierce in tight for a hug. "I'm so proud of you!"

"I had no idea you knew how to do any of that," Cade said as he took in the implications of Pierce's invention.

"I learned from all of you," Pierce said with a shy smile.

"You better keep us in mind for your first sale!" Morgan smiled as she embraced her new brother-in-law in a hug.

"And you all need to be on your honeymoon," Pierce said. The mood of excitement suddenly shifted as everyone remembered the reason Miles and Morgan were still in Keeneston.

"We're not going anywhere when you're in trouble. Right, Morgan?" Miles more stated than asked as he slipped his arm around his new bride.

"That's right. Besides, I can't wait to stand in front of the media and lambaste them for casting doubt on your character. I'm going to love it, in fact," Morgan said with a sly grin. His newest sister-in-law had a feisty side, and he didn't doubt for one second that Morgan would do whatever it took to help him.

"Do you think the Cropbot had anything to do with Dr. Oldham's death?" Marshall asked after a minute.

"It's the only reason I can think of. The patent application is in my name as I was the inventor, but I signed a contract with Dr. Oldham saying I'd give him five percent of the sales for five years as consideration for all his help. But, as I said, all these documents are in a lock box at the bank." Pierce wrapped the wet towel around his neck and watched as the fire department started to beat back the flames.

"Maybe Mrs. Oldham and Aiden don't know about the deal or the documents and think that if they just eliminated you both, they would have a clear path to the patent," Marshall speculated.

"We'll talk about it more later," Miles said as he straightened and turned to face the sound of cars coming up the dirt drive from the main road about a quarter mile away. "Now, we have company. Lots of it."

CHAPTER SEVEN

Tammy took a seat on the tailgate of Will's massive Ford truck as the town descended on them. Kenna and Will were the first to arrive, followed by the Rose sisters, and then John Wolfe who shot an annoyed expression at being beaten there by the Rose sisters. Bridget arrived with Marko in tow. Finally Mo appeared with a new royal bodyguard tagging along. Henry had shown up in his suit, but he'd looked rumpled and his hair was messed. Mo showed up in the early morning looking like he just stepped off the pages of *GQ*.

The town had pulled their cars and trucks around each other and tailgates were lowered as everyone took a seat to hear Pierce tell what happened. Tammy gave a weak smile as Ahmed appeared out of the darkness next to the truck she was sitting in.

"How are you doing, my dear?" Ahmed asked quietly.

"Tired. But, I'm glad you snuck over here. I have something I want to run by you," she whispered.

"What is it?" Ahmed asked smoothly as he took the seat next to her. Oh boy. Tammy knew it was Pierce with a hold on her heart, but the erotic smell coming from Ahmed's coat and the feel of his strong, warm body next to her was enough to make any girl question her heart.

Tammy told Ahmed about her trip downtown and about the two people who drove Pierce home. Then she told him about the car that almost hit her on the way out to the farm. "I think someone is trying to frame Pierce."

Ahmed only nodded his head and then jumped down from the truck. Tammy looked up and saw that Bridget was making her way over to Mo. "Your Highness. It's so nice to see you again. I don't know if you remember me…"

"Of course I do, Miss Springer." Mo purred in his smoothest accent. So, Bridget knew Mo? Obviously she didn't know him enough to call him Mo like everyone in town, Tammy thought as she watched him shake hands with Bridget.

"Miss Springer, may I introduce you to my head of security, Ahmed." Mo held out his arm and Ahmed stepped forward with a silent nod of his head. "Ahmed, Miss Springer was in charge of my security in Belgium when you stayed with Dani." Again, Ahmed just gave the slightest nod of his head as an indication that he had heard Mo.

Bridget held out her hand and looked Ahmed in the eyes. "It's so nice to meet you in person. I've heard a lot of things about you and I'm sure your reputation precedes you."

Ahmed shook her hand and then with another nod turned and headed for Marshall. Tammy watched as they talked quietly for a moment. Marshall nodded and called Annie, Noodle, and Dinky over to talk while Ahmed made his way over to where the fire department was cleaning up. The fire had been extinguished. The back half of the house was destroyed and the living room was damaged, but they had been able to save most of it.

"Attention! I've learned some new evidence. Pierce, you may want to hear this." Marshall called out. People immediately quieted down and stepped closer as Marshall told them about Tammy's trip downtown and also the car she saw speeding away.

"It's not concrete, but it's too much of a coincidence for me. Two people carry Pierce out of a bar and Tammy sees two people speeding away from here. If you've seen anything, please report it to me immediately," ordered Marshall.

"We'll keep our eyes peeled, won't we, ladies?" Miss Lily said as her sisters nodded their heads in agreement. Within seconds, the crowd was in a gossip frenzy.

Pierce made his way to where Tammy still sat covered in Ahmed's black suit coat. He wanted to rip it off of her, but all he had to offer her was a wet towel. Most of his clothes were burnt to a crisp.

"Tammy, I don't know what to say." He stopped before her and had to stifle the impulse to step between her legs, which she was so enticingly dangling off the tailgate.

"It's nothing. You'd do the same for me," Tammy said with a tired smile. Her words froze Pierce in place. Would he have done the same? He knew he would now, but a year ago? A year ago he'd been a selfish jerk. But, now he could make up for it.

"Tammy…"

"Tammy, Pierce, we're going to head back and get ready for the breakfast crowd. We'll do everything we can," Miss Daisy said as she and her sisters gave both her and Pierce hugs before heading back to town.

Everyone was ready to head home for a quick nap before the start of the day. Pierce was starting to feel anxious. He needed time with Tammy. He needed to talk to her, to thank her again and again.

"Well, I better get home, too. I'm exhausted," Tammy said as she slid off Will's truck as he and Kenna got in to head home.

"No, wait!" Pierce said anxiously. He stepped forward and looked down at her. She barely made it up to his chin, but it looked like she'd fit perfectly in his arms. Her large round blue eyes drew him in. His hands cupped her small rounded hips as he gently pulled her nearer.

"Hey, Pierce!" Paige called out. Tammy jumped back and the moment was lost.

"What is it, dear sister?" Pierce asked innocently when what he really wanted to do was grab Tammy and kiss her senseless.

"Cole and I were talking. Instead of going back to Mom's, why don't you take the apartment above Southern Charms?" Paige asked, completely ignoring her brother's annoyance.

"Thank you for offering to let me stay above your shop," Pierce said.

Tammy didn't know what to make of the situation. She was so confused, excited, and tired at the same time. As much as she wanted that kiss, Tammy only wanted it when he wanted her. Not because he was thankful. She wanted him overtaken with passion and right now with his brother-in-law and sister standing there was not that time. With a little wave to Cole, she snuck to her car and headed back to her apartment.

Pierce thanked his sister and grabbed the key to the apartment. He wanted to make sure Tammy got home safe and sound. As he hurried to his truck and was about to take off, his phone rang. He looked at the caller ID and read that the number was blocked.

"Hey. Where are you?" Pierce asked when he answered the phone.

"I'm in Russia for work, which luckily entails drinking a lot of vodka," his brother's rough voice said over the phone.

"Someday you'll tell me what you do. Drinking vodka in Russia, skiing in Switzerland, surfing in the Pacific. I want that job, Cy."

"It's more taxing than you think. I'm always so far away when my brothers need me. Now, what's going on and how can I help?"

Pierce filled Cy in on his invention, finding Dr. Oldham dead, the memory loss, and finally the fire. Pierce also told Cy all about how Tammy rescued him and the investigation she did downtown that night.

"I'm so sorry I'm away, but it sounds like you have someone looking out for you. I'll be home in a heartbeat if you need me," Pierce heard his brother say with a hint of regret in his voice.

"It's okay, Cy. I'll call you and let you know if I need you. Enjoy your vodka and women," Pierce joked before getting serious again. "Hopefully, with this new information, we'll be able to prove my innocence. Something good is bound to happen soon. I can only take so much more."

"It sounds like something good has already happened," Cy said mysteriously as Pierce pulled to a stop by Southern Charms. He watched Tammy's taillights disappear down the street.

"What good thing could possibly have happened?" Pierce asked in disbelief as he walked up the back steps to Paige's old apartment.

Cy laughed and then told him, "That you finally got your head out of your ass and realize how amazing Tammy is. She's a spitfire in the best possible way. She's smart, loyal, sweet, carries a knife, heroically saves your life, and is pretty damn hot to boot."

Pierce groaned. He knew everything Cy said was true. He's been realizing it over the past days and now he felt terrible. "It's too late now. I've lost my chance. She has this Greek boyfriend now. He had his hands all over her at the wedding this weekend."

"I don't like telling you to break them up, but I think you need to realize two things. One, she wouldn't be doing all this if she didn't still have feelings for you, and I'm guessing the boyfriend will soon be an ex-boyfriend the more time she spends with you. Second, she's been yours for two years. Now you need to go claim her before someone else does… or until I get home," Cy said cockily, giving a little laugh when he heard Pierce curse under his breath.

As Cy laughed, Pierce thought about what his brother said. Cy was right. Tammy was his and he'd waited long enough to make the move. Greek boyfriend or not, he was going to fight for Tammy for one simple reason—she was worth it.

After talking with Cy, Pierce jumped into the shower and quickly washed off. He found some jeans and a t-shirt of Cole's and slipped them on. The early morning light cast a warm glow on downtown as he hurried toward Tammy's apartment. The smell of muffins reached his nose as he neared the Blossom Café. The front door was open and he could hear Miss Daisy talking with Miss Violet.

Pierce rounded the building and slowly made his way to the equally open back door. He had to wait until Miss Violet started washing dishes before he could sneak up the stairs to Tammy's apartment. He knocked softly and rubbed his hands on his jeans when he heard her soft footfalls approach the door.

Tammy had driven home while a battle raged in her mind. Would Pierce have kissed her if she hadn't left? Was Pierce even going to kiss her? It was too much. She shook her head. If it were meant to be, it would have happened by now. She had already sacrificed Demetri. It was time to grow up and end this fascination.

Tammy tried to push it from her mind as she had stood under the hot spray in her shower. After scrubbing herself clean, she finally felt like herself again. She had slipped into a pink camisole nightshirt with matching shorts and was heading to bed when she heard a soft knock at the door.

Figuring Miss Violet was sending up some breakfast, Tammy didn't bother with her robe and just opened the door. She instantly started breathing heavily when she saw Pierce leaning against the doorframe. He had showered and was wearing a black shirt that looked to be painted across his chest and shoulders. His jeans hugged his thighs and suddenly Tammy had a whole series of very naughty thoughts go through her mind. Way to grow up, she thought.

"Pierce!" Tammy gasped. "What are you doing here?"

"I didn't get my kiss." Pierce leaned down and captured her lips in his.

Tammy's head fell back as she let him ravish her mouth. His lips were soft and melded to hers with confidence as Pierce stoked the fire within her. She shuddered as Pierce cupped her face in his hand and deepened the kiss.

Pierce pulled away way too soon. He left with a smile that said it all. Tammy was rooted to the floor and watched with a mixture of confusion and utter satisfaction as his perfectly shaped bottom faded from view.

Pierce made his way home with a new sense of clarity. Any reason he had in the past for keeping his distance from Tammy was shattered with that kiss. He enjoyed a minute of pure male satisfaction before sliding into bed as he remembered the way Tammy looked after he kissed her senseless. Tonight, his dreams would be good.

CHAPTER EIGHT

Tammy tapped her fingers on her desk. The computer monitor glowed in front of her as she contemplated what she felt for Pierce. That kiss changed everything. She knew they had chemistry, but it was only superficial before. She had been attracted to him for two years, but even she knew there was a difference between falling in lust and falling in love. Now that she'd been around him during his worst time, seeing how he handled it, and then how he kissed her—wow. Lust grew up and became love in that split second. And right when she had decided it was never meant to be. Tammy groaned and gently banged her head against her desk. What was she going to do?

"What do you think she's doing?" Kenna asked Dani not so quietly from the doorway to the offices as the two women stared at Tammy banging her head.

"I don't know, but I'd be willing to bet a man was behind it. What else can drive a woman so nuts?" Dani joked as they walked to her desk.

"Oh hush. You two are happily married women and know nothing about being single anymore. It's painful," Tammy sighed.

"Maybe it wouldn't be if you stopped banging your head," Kenna said dryly. "What's Pierce done now?"

"Who said it was about Pierce?" Sassy Tammy made an appearance and then quickly went away as both Dani and Kenna gave her a "yeah, right" look.

"Okay, it's Pierce."

The bell over the door tinkled as Bridget and Annie walked in. Tammy froze and everyone turned to see who had just walked in. "Oh, it's just Bridget and Annie. They'll be able to help," Kenna said as she urged Tammy to continue.

"Help with what?" Bridget asked suspiciously.

"She needs advice on men. You work with nothing but men; you'll be able to give Tammy some great insight." Kenna started to sound too optimistic for Tammy and the desire to bang her head against the desk returned.

"Ha. I worked with alpha men—the only way to deal with them was to be an alpha, too. Confident and never giving ground when you know you're right. Lots of hard work, studying, and practicing to not only be their equal, but to be better than they were was also involved. I have to be so careful to never be accused of sleeping my way to the top. Hell, I haven't worn a dress since the Presidential Inaugural Ball. So, I may learn something here, too." Bridget sat on the edge of Tammy's desk and leaned forward.

"So, what did Pierce do or not do?" Dani asked as she lowered herself into one of the office chairs.

"Well, y'all know he's ignored me for years and then last night he showed up at my door and kissed me. I mean, *kissed* me," Tammy sighed as she remembered the feel of his lips on her.

"Then what did he do?" Kenna, Dani, and Bridget asked at the same time.

"He left. Just turned around and left," Tammy told them. Upon seeing their expressions, Tammy felt better about her confusion. "So what do I do now?"

"Hmm. What about a little makeover to help him realize what he'd be missing if he walked away," Kenna suggested.

"That's a horrible idea."

The women turned and saw Henry leaning against the arch heading back to the offices. "As if you would know. You'll probably tell her to say, 'Are you Superman, because you have buns of steel!'" Dani laughed.

"Or, 'do you work for UPS, because I have a package for you.'" Kenna wiped a tear from her eye as they all laughed. Henry wasn't one to give relationship advice unless that advice included the worst pick-up lines you'd ever heard.

As he joined the women around Tammy's desk, Henry continued. "Go ahead and laugh it up. But no, I wasn't going to suggest those great lines. I don't think they'd work on Pierce. Instead I was going to tell you to act as if nothing happened."

"Why would I do that?" Tammy asked as they all turned to look at Henry.

"It'll drive him crazy. If he kissed you the way you said and left like that, he did it for impact. He wants you off balance. You pretend it didn't happen and he'll think maybe he isn't as good as he thinks and will do anything to prove that he is."

"Wow. That's kinda genius. How did you come up with that?" Tammy asked him.

"Women. You think men are so hard to understand. We're simple. Everything revolves around wanting sex. The more you act like you don't want it, the more of a challenge it becomes to make sure we have sex with you. See, simple. You all are the complicated ones."

The chime above the door tinkled and the object of their discussion walked in. Pierce stopped and Tammy cringed as she realized everyone had turned around and stared at him. She never thought she'd ever say this, but she was going to take Henry's advice. She gave Pierce a quick smile and then went back to looking at the computer screen.

"Um, I got a call you wanted to see me?" Pierce asked when no one said anything.

Tammy looked up and saw that Pierce was looking straight at her. "Oh! I didn't call you." She smiled when she saw his smirk fade. "Henry did." Tammy lowered her head again and stared at the blank screen, willing herself not to vault over the table and rip his clothes off.

"That's right. Marshall and Annie have been talking with Detectives Basher and Cowell—unofficially, of course. The detectives want to meet with you along with the special prosecutor. Is that alright with you?" Henry pulled out his phone and looked at the calendar. "How's eleven?"

"Of course. Do they realize they got the wrong guy?" Pierce asked hopefully.

"No. But they are now at least willing to listen to what we have to say. That fire may be the best thing to happen to you."

Pierce sat in the lobby of the police station in silence. He had to admit he didn't really know how to express how he was feeling. He thought for sure Tammy would be flustered to see him. At the very least come on strong like she always did before. Was it really unreasonable to think she'd get up and give him a kiss hello? One second he was a strutting stallion and the next he was a gelding. She had acted like the kiss hadn't meant anything. Was he not as good as he thought? Well then, he would just have to show Tammy how good he could be.

"Pierce?"

"Hm?" Pierce finally looked over at Henry.

"They're ready for us. You okay?" Pierce nodded and followed Henry into a conference room. Detective Basher and Mr. Hickson were sitting at the table while Detective Cowell prowled around the room.

"Thank you for seeing us. As Sheriff Davies told you, there've been some new developments," Henry said as he shook all their hands.

Mr. Hickson pulled out a pen and paper somewhere from the depths of a huge bag he had with him. Pierce was surprised he was even an attorney. He looked like a rumpled mess.

"Mr. Davies, this is all 'off the record,' so to say. Your brother and your attorney have made a pressing case for your innocence. While every criminal I know says he's innocent, I always listen." Detective Cowell snorted and Mr. Hickson ignored him. "Tell me what these new developments are."

Pierce told them about the intruders, the fire, and then what Tammy found. Henry then informed them of the lawsuit regarding Pierce's invention. Detective Basher kept a blank face and took notes of his own. Detective Cowell continually snorted and laughed while Mr. Hickson's expression constantly changed.

"Well, that is interesting, Mr. Davies. If what you're saying is true, then it would give me reason to explore other options. However, that's all circumstantial. I want hard evidence before I'm swayed completely. You, Mr. Davies, need the DNA test to come back in your favor and for your memory to return so that you can fill in a whole heck of a lot of blanks from that night," Mr. Hickson told him as he put his pad away.

Henry leaned back in his chair and finished reading a text message. "My paralegal is at the bar now. She says the witness is there and willing to talk to you. I suggest we go and see if being there triggers anything. It'll also give you a chance to evaluate him as a witness."

They all looked at each other, and then at Mr. Hickson's nod, Detective Basher agreed.

"Come on! This is just a wild goose chase. A red herring! We have the real killer right here." Cowell spat.

"One thing you need to learn is that you follow up on every lead. You don't want to know the feeling of putting an innocent man behind bars. Trust me." Basher got up and opened the door for Pierce and Henry. "Let's go."

Mr. Hickson scribbled in his notebook as Basher and Cowell questioned the waiter. Pierce stood in the middle of the room and then instinctively went to a seat. "That's where you were sitting the other night," the waiter called out.

"I remember," Pierce muttered as he sat down in the chair. "I ordered two fingers of bourbon."

"That's right. You did," The waiter called out as everyone moved closer to Pierce. They all stood quietly by Pierce waiting to see if he remembered anything else.

"I remember one man, but he's all blurry. Everything is blurry and cloaked in shadows except that glass of bourbon I was drinking. I just remember a man taking a seat next to me and trying to talk to me." Pierce shook his head, pulling himself out of the past.

"That's great, Pierce. See, your memories can come back!" Tammy said excitedly, ignoring Henry's suggestion to play it cool as she rushed over to his side.

"I think I have heard enough, Mr. Davies." Mr. Hickson opened his bag to put away his notebook as pieces of paper fell out. Mr. Hickson shoved his glasses up his pudgy nose and crammed the papers into his bag. "Detective Basher, would you call to check on the status of the DNA test. Put a rush on it if they haven't started it yet. Mr. Davies, I don't know if you're innocent or just one heck of a good liar, but there's one way to find out. When you regain your memory and the DNA comes back, we'll have the whole story in front of us. But for now, you're still our prime suspect and subject to the restrictions of your bond agreement."

With a nod, Mr. Hickson turned and walked out. Tammy looked to Henry and he just shrugged as the detectives scrambled to catch up with the disheveled prosecutor. Henry thanked the waiter and they all walked out to the parking lot. Pierce's black pick-up truck was parked next to Henry's sports car and Tammy stood still. She should go with Henry and see if he needed any help with the case, but her heart longed to be next to Pierce in his truck.

Henry opened the passenger door for her, but then he paused. Tammy looked over her shoulder and saw Pierce shoot him a look. Henry then closed the door and cleared his throat. "Um, I have some errands to run. It's getting late and I want to get them done before the stores close. Pierce, could you take Tammy home for me?"

"Oh," Pierce said with the worst case of fake surprise Tammy had ever heard. "Sure, I guess I can do that."

Tammy rolled her eyes when she really wanted to jump up and down. So, Henry made inappropriate comments and had the worst pick-up lines she'd ever heard, but deep down he was a good guy who looked out for her.

Pierce opened the door and waited for Tammy to get into his truck. She climbed in and then ran her fingers through her hair and applied some light pink lip gloss she'd bought at the grocery store before Pierce made it around to his side of the driver's side of the truck.

"So, I don't think I've thanked you for all you've done for me today. I don't know what I'd do without you, Tammy," Pierce said with a deep sincerity in his voice.

Tammy felt herself blush as she looked down at her skirt to try to keep him from noticing. "You're welcome. It's my job."

"Your job? Tammy, I'm just a job?" Pierce asked slowly.

Tammy could hear the hurt in his voice. "You know you're not. But we also know that I'm just the flavor of the moment for you. You've never paid me any attention and the only reason you are now is because I'm helping you." Tammy had to get it out there. Suddenly she felt strong enough to finally know the answer. She raised her head and looked at Pierce. The well-shaped jaw, the short stubble covering his face, and his hazel eyes flashing. He looked relaxed, but she knew he wasn't.

"It's true, Tammy. I never did pay you enough attention, but that doesn't mean I didn't know you were there. You were too nice. Too good. And I wasn't grown up enough to realize that you were also the type of woman I should've been paying attention to. Then in one kiss, the last two years slapped me in the face." Pierce smiled to hide his embarrassment and then gave her a wink.

Tammy laughed and felt the tension ease. She had just found her confidence and suddenly she felt like a teenager again. But then she remembered talking to Bridget and how she had to earn the respect of the men she worked with and she did that by not backing down. Confident Tammy returned and she kept her eyes on Pierce, refusing to look back down at her clasped hands resting in her lap.

"But," Pierce started before glancing quickly at her with a wicked grin on his face, "it appears that our kiss didn't affect you as it did me."

"Well, then maybe you don't know me like you think you do. It seems to me that we both think we know each other when we really don't." Tammy looked and saw the freshly painted Keeneston water tower off in the distance. Their time was coming to an end too soon. No matter how bad she wanted to be Confident Tammy, she needed Pierce to be the one to come to her after all these years of chasing him.

"Well, I know a way to get to know each other better," Pierce winked and Tammy laughed as she gave him a swat. "No, no,

I really do. It's almost six; how about I take you out to dinner at the café? I'll even walk you home."

"Are you asking me out on a date?" Tammy's breath caught as she tried to keep from bouncing up and down in her seat with excitement.

Pierce chuckled. "Yes, that's typically what a man means when he asks a woman to have dinner with him."

"At the café? Everyone will talk," she warned.

"Tammy, are you trying to talk me out of asking you out?" Pierce teased as he pulled onto Main Street.

"No! I just wanted to make sure you knew what you were getting yourself into. Dinner sounds great." Tammy noticed she was bouncing her knee in excitement. She took a breath and told herself to act like she'd been on a date before. Of course she had, just not with her dream guy whom she measured every other date against!

CHAPTER NINE

Pierce opened the door to the café and Tammy walked in. She paused as she waited for him to come to her side. She looked around as she waited for the heads to turn and whispers to start, but so far no one seemed to notice.

Tammy almost jumped when she felt Pierce's warm, strong hand settle on the middle of her back and gently urge her forward to an empty table right in the middle of the café. Pierce held out the chair and Tammy took a seat. Still, no one paid too much attention until Pierce trailed his hand from Tammy's shoulder and across her back as he moved around her toward his chair.

Miss Daisy appeared a second later with her notepad and reached for a pen from the midst of her hair bun. "What brings you two in tonight?" she asked skeptically.

Here it is. Tammy noticed the heads turning and the sudden quiet that overtook the normally noisy café. She had seen it happen time after time. It was almost as if you weren't a real couple until you had dinner at the café to make it official.

"Tammy finally agreed to have dinner with me."

Tammy tried not to cringe. He said that really loud, didn't he?

"A date?" Miss Daisy asked suspiciously. The whispers started and Tammy's face turned bright red. Okay, she'd never do this to anyone again.

"About darn time!"

Tammy's eyes widened as she whipped her head around. "Father James?"

The old priest shrugged his shoulders and went back to eating.

"Humph. So, what would you like for dinner?" Miss Daisy asked as all the other patrons went back to their dinners.

"Pecan chicken, please," Tammy ordered as she looked around the café. No one was paying any attention.

"Fried catfish please, Miss Daisy." Pierce waited until Miss Daisy handed off the order to Miss Violet and then turned back to Tammy. "Was it just me, or was that anticlimactic?"

"It was, but it was plenty for me. I'm never going to stop and stare at people again!"

"Well, at least I don't have to worry about everyone listening while I try to get to know you better. Don't tell anyone, but I may even try to make a move," Pierce whispered as he reached out and pulled Tammy's hand into his. "Now, let's get to know each other."

Pierce had never been on such a rollercoaster ride before. When he had asked Tammy about her childhood, his stomach fell as she told him about her father and his drinking. Her mother had long left him by the time she reached high school. Guilt washed over him as he remembered hearing about "Trailer Park Tammy" and her drunk of a father but never gave it much thought. He hadn't even known that her father died one week before she turned eighteen and that she had been supporting herself since she was fourteen.

But then she laughed when he told her how he'd sneak out of the house and follow his four older brothers around when they went to parties. All the while he thought he was so sneaky only to find out when he got older his brothers knew he was there every time. He felt as if he was on the top of the world when she broke out laughing at his story of how he rescued Gus and his parrot's obsession with stealing snacks. She giggled when he told her Gus would climb off his cage, waddle across the floor, and pull himself up to the kitchen table with his beak to steal cookies off the plate.

"What did you do when you caught him?" Tammy asked as she giggled again.

"Put them in Tupperware!"

"Poor bird. Being deprived of his cookies."

"Don't worry about him. I came home and found the lid laying on the floor and two cookies missing. I looked over at him, he blinked, and said 'Aw, that's a good bird!'" Pierce smiled as Tammy laughed. God, she was so gorgeous. She was full of spunk, and happiness radiated from her.

"Well, dinner was wonderful. Thank you, Pierce." Tammy set her napkin on the table and Pierce suddenly felt nervous. It was time to take her home. Could he do better this time with the kiss? He was sure going to try!

"You're welcome. It was all my pleasure. Let me walk you home." Pierce winked and held out his arm for her to take.

"Why, thank you!" Tammy said between laughter. "I usually cut through the kitchen."

Pierce led her around the table and was about to walk through the door into the kitchen when Miss Violet whipped out her wooden spoon faster than a lightning bolt and smacked him on the arm.

"Ow! What was that for?" Pierce asked as he rubbed his arm and looked down at the angelic face of the plump woman before him.

"Do you think I was born yesterday? I'm not about to allow the fox into the henhouse. Now scoot." Miss Violet waved her spoon at him as he chuckled. He wasn't happy. He'd been thinking about kissing Tammy all night, but Miss Violet in a tizzy was funny enough to crack him up. With her white hair bobbing and apron flapping, she pushed him out of the kitchen.

"Fine." Pierce held up his hands in surrender. "I'll go, don't hurt me."

"Thank you for dinner, Pierce. It was a really great time." Tammy smiled and Pierce felt it in his heart.

"Good night, Tammy." Pierce rocked back on his heels and sent her his sexiest smile as he watched her head upstairs, all the while thinking how to sneak past the Rose sisters to get his kiss good-night.

"I need to talk to you after you put your tongue back into your mouth."

Pierce whipped around and saw the retreating form of Ahmed. How did he do that? He hadn't heard a thing!

Pierce gave up on sneaking upstairs for the moment and followed Ahmed outside. Ahmed was a friend. But when he spoke like that, Pierce got a little worried. He wasn't saying Ahmed would make him disappear, but he didn't necessarily feel certain of that fact.

"What's going on?" he asked as he caught up with Ahmed out on the sidewalk.

"There's one thing we need to discuss before I can continue."

Pierce felt a shiver go through him at Ahmed's deadly serious tone. "Sure. What is it?" he asked nervously.

"Tammy is a sweet and innocent girl who makes me laugh." Pierce couldn't stop his eyebrow from shooting up, "Okay, she makes me *think* about laughing." Ahmed straightened and uncrossed his arms from his chest.

"If you hurt her," Ahmed poked him in the chest and Pierce had to stop himself from rubbing the spot, "I'll hurt you. Got it?"

Pierce gulped and nodded. "I understand you completely."

"Good." Ahmed relaxed, well, as much as Ahmed could relax. "Now, I've been looking into your invention. Who else knew about it?"

"No one. Dr. Oldham and I knew the implications and decided not to tell anyone. We weren't even going to tell our families. Why?"

"I found something on the professor's computer," Ahmed said smoothly.

"How'd you see Dr. Oldham's computer?" Pierce asked and then had to shrug when Ahmed simply looked at him. "Okay, stupid question. What did you find?"

"Someone was watching every stroke that was entered. It's called ghosting. Someone else knew about the discovery."

"Who? And do you think they're responsible for Dr. Oldham's death?" Pierce asked excitedly. If that person did it, then Pierce could finally breathe. Pierce knew he could kill someone under the right circumstances. After all, he had done so when Miles's life was on the line. But he couldn't imagine killing someone who was innocent. Unfortunately, he didn't really know if he did or didn't.

"I think there's a good chance of it. It appears to all come back to your invention. I'll know who was ghosting soon and will let you know."

Just as fast as he was there, Ahmed disappeared into the shadows of the night. After the talk with Ahmed, Pierce determined he'd much rather be on his good side than bad. Maybe his goodnight kiss would just have to wait.

Tammy sat on her couch and stared at the clock. The café closed at nine and it was nine-thirty now. The sisters lived right down the street, but she was pretty sure they were still downstairs cleaning. Any minute now they'd lock up and head down the sidewalk. That's when she'd make her move. The hand on her clock moved. Nine thirty-one. She'd been waiting for two hours now and each minute seemed like an eternity.

Tammy had been sitting on her couch ever since she came back upstairs. The dinner was wonderful. She felt so good really being honest with someone. And the little touches! They had driven her wild. A brush of his knee, the holding of her hand, the way he placed his hand on her back to walk her through the crowd. Tammy sighed. By the end of the dinner, her body was sizzling with need and her thoughts were firmly set on the kiss she knew was coming. But then it didn't happen.

Fairy godmothers, her hiney. They sure as heck didn't grant her wish tonight. Which was why she was going to grant it herself, just as soon as they headed home. Tammy felt the time was right. She stripped out of her clothes and pulled on some black yoga pants and a black spandex shirt she used for working out. Feeling like a thief in the night, she waited until she heard Miss Daisy and Miss Violet twittering away on the sidewalk as they locked up.

Tammy hurried down the back stairs and kept to the shadows as she made her way toward Southern Charms. It took no time at all to find herself standing at the bottom of the old stairs leading to the private apartment above Paige's store. She took a breath to steady her jumpy nerves and headed up the stairs.

At the landing, Tammy looked through the kitchen window and saw Pierce standing at the counter. He was shirtless and wearing only the athletic shorts from the other night and tennis shoes. He looked to be shining as he drank a glass of water. Tammy sighed. He must've just finished a run. Who needed fairy godmothers to keep her from this? Sun-kissed skin, muscular arms, trim legs, strong chest lightly covered with light brown hair that trailed down his abs straight to… Pierce turned and their eyes connected. Tammy jumped back with embarrassment as she was caught. One foot slipped off the narrow landing, causing her arms to pinwheel as she reached out to grab anything to keep her from falling down the stairs.

Strong arms encircled her. "I got you!" Pierce pulled her tight against him as he stepped into the kitchen. "Better?" he asked with a chuckle.

"Sorry! I, um, tripped right as I got to the top." Tammy's hand brushed against Pierce's chest as she tucked her side bangs behind her ear. Confident Tammy surged forward at the feel and closeness of Pierce. Deciding to take a chance, Tammy placed her hand on his chest and looked up at him. "Thanks for saving me," she said in her most seductive voice.

Pierce froze and looked down at her hand. He appeared to be thinking of something as he stepped back. "So, what brings you to my temporary place?"

"Aw, nookie!" Gus sang from where he was dancing on his perch.

Tammy's eyes widened and she turned bright red. Gus laughed and Tammy started wishing she had fallen down the stairs instead.

"Sorry. He can't say the letter *C* very well. He just wants a cookie," Pierce explained as he reached into the cabinet for a bird snack. "I'm glad you stopped by, actually. It was really nice to talk to you over dinner. I'm a mess, but why don't you give me just a minute to jump in the shower and then we can watch a movie. I can't promise there's anything good, but it would be nice just to be with you for a while."

"A movie sounds great." Tammy's imagination ran wild—sitting on the couch with Pierce's arm around her, then he'd kiss her quickly to test the waters, and then Confident Tammy would jump him for hot couch sex. Yeah, that sounded good to her.

"Perfect." Pierce's sexy smile shot straight to her. "The movies are by the TV. Why don't you pick one out? I'll be back in just a minute," Pierce said interrupting her thoughts.

"Will do." Tammy watched as he headed back to the master bedroom and stood rooted to the floor in debate. Was the whole shower an act to have her thinking about him naked? If so, it was working. Or was she really supposed to pick out a movie and watch it with him? She could see two little Tammys on her shoulder. The good one urged her to pick a movie. The bad one suggested she follow Pierce into the shower.

"Well, it would only be good manners to help him wash his back," Tammy said as she slipped out of her tennis shoes and padded across the floor toward the back rooms, envisioning something else hot and steamy besides the shower.

She paused with her pants halfway down her legs. The only thing stopping her from climbing completely naked into the shower just down the hall was that she could've sworn she heard a knock on the door. Tammy stood frozen with her pants around her calves. No, that couldn't have been a knock. It had to be her heart beating. She was so close… *knock, knock.* Dammit! That was a knock!

Tammy pulled up her pants just as the bathroom door opened. "Just a second!" Pierce shouted as he ran out of the bathroom wearing nothing but a towel. His body still wet with the spray and a good amount of well-muscled thigh showed as he hurried past her to open the back door.

"Hey, sis, Cole. What are you doing here?" Tammy heard him ask from the kitchen.

"We came to bring you groceries. Here, hold your nephew while I put them away." Pierce stood frozen in place. "Pierce, can you move out of the doorway, please?" Paige's annoyed voice reached her and she wondered if she had enough time to hide in the bedroom.

"Now's not the best time," Pierce said as he grabbed the baby being thrust upon him.

"Yeah, yeah, you just got out of the shower. I see that, but you'll live," Paige pushed past him and came face to face with Tammy standing in the living room. "Oh! Now I see why it's not a good time. I'm interrupting."

"Oh, no! No! I was, um, just leaving," Tammy said as she slipped on her tennis shoes.

"No, you're not," Pierce said as Ryan chewed on his finger with joy. "We were just getting ready to watch a movie."

"Yes, please stay. Paige and I were just dropping off these groceries and wanted to check in on Pierce. It seems he's being well taken care of," Cole said. The black cowboy hat hid his eyes as Tammy tried to decide if he was being serious or if he was teasing her.

"In a minute, Cole. I wanted to talk to my little brother for a second." Paige sat down on the couch and smiled serenely.

"Well, it's been a long day. I'm going to get back to my place. Good night, everyone." Tammy slipped out the back door as fast as she could. She heard Pierce calling after her but was too embarrassed to stop until she reached her apartment.

"That was uncalled for. Geez, Paige, I had a nice night planned and you ruined it." Pierce glared as his sister.

"Karma's a beautiful thing, isn't she?" Paige laughed.

"Karma? I never did anything like this to you." Pierce stopped and remembered him and his brothers doing the exact same thing to Cole here when he and Paige first got together. "Okay, maybe I did. Now that you have my undivided attention, what did you need?"

"Nothing. We were just dropping off the groceries before putting Ryan to bed. But, now that you're here and we're in private, there is something I wouldn't mind telling you," Paige said as Ryan decided to try to chew on his shoulder instead.

"Yes?"

"I like Tammy. A lot. In fact, as much as I love you, I think she may be too good for you after the way you treated her. So, whatever you do, don't screw this up."

Pierce handed Cole the baby who was instantly engrossed with trying to reach his daddy's hat to chew on. "Why does everyone think I'll screw this up?"

"Maybe because you managed to screw it up for the last two years," Cole said sarcastically.

"Way to be on my side!" Cole shrugged at Pierce as Paige simply looked at him. He knew his brother-in-law was right. "Well, maybe I wasn't ready then."

"And you are now? Are you really ready for what Tammy needs now? Serious, long-term relationship that might include," Paige gasped, "the *M* word?"

Pierce stood quietly as he processed his sister's words. Marriage. To Tammy? To anyone? Was he ready for that?

"That's what I thought. Good night, Pierce." Paige gave him a kiss on the cheek and Cole gave him a nod as they both headed out the kitchen door and back to their house across the street.

Pierce turned off the lights and made his way back to the bedroom. He tossed the towel into the bathroom and climbed into bed. There was only one thing he knew deep down. He was ready for everything his sister had said—for a relationship and for marriage with Tammy. God! Just don't let his mother find out. He wanted to do it his own way. Satisfaction and a calm of knowing it was right settled on him as he drifted off to sleep.

CHAPTER TEN

Tammy rolled out of bed and groaned. She had had a couple of glasses of wine after returning from Pierce's apartment last night. She looked at the nightstand, okay, most of the bottle. What she needed now was a hot shower and a clear head. Unfortunately, the thought of a hot shower only reminded her of last night.

She turned on her shower, brushed her teeth, and undressed. How big of a fool had she made of herself last night? Ah, the shower felt so good. She rested her head against the wall and let the water wash away all her fears. She was a strong, independent woman and she hadn't needed a man to take care of her before, so why sweat the small stuff like what his family thinks of her?

Feeling better, Tammy turned off the water and pushed aside the shower curtain. Tammy screamed and hid behind the curtain as she saw a figure in black leaning against the doorframe.

"What are you doing here?" she screamed as she tried to calm down.

Ahmed tossed her a towel but didn't move. "I found something."

"How did you get in here?"

Ahmed just looked at her.

"Okay, but did anyone see you?" Tammy rolled her eyes when Ahmed simply raised an eyebrow. "Don't be so confident. I know you're a sexy, badass something or other, but Miss Violet and Miss Daisy have more than thirty years of experience on you and

I'd hate to be in your shoes if they caught you here. Ever been hit with a skillet?" Tammy asked as she wrapped the towel around her.

"I'll try to be elusive," Ahmed said dryly.

"Did you make a joke?" Tammy teased. When Ahmed didn't smile back, she just rolled her eyes at him again and got out of the shower. "You know, there was a time when I dreamed about being naked with you."

"But then Pierce walked into your life and I never play second to anyone."

"Humph. I can believe that. So, what did you find?"

"The reason Pierce's memory is gone."

Tammy sat snuggled into the luxurious seats of Ahmed's new black McLaren. Being head of security for a prince sure paid off. They turned onto the dirt road leading to the back of the Davies's farm and Tammy watched as they drove past the white farmhouse and past the fields of crops until they reached the back barn. There was a small, rectangular fenced-in area attached to the barn and a small circular patch of grass. That's where Tammy saw Pierce. She gasped and her hand flew to her mouth as Pierce climbed the fence in the small holding stall. A massive bull stood restlessly shifting from foot to foot on the other side of the fence from Pierce.

The second Ahmed had stopped the car, Tammy raced to where Cade stood with one booted foot on the lower fence board watching his brother. Cade seemed so calm with his baseball hat pulled low to shield his eyes from the sun.

"What is he doing?" Tammy asked fearfully as she slid to a stop next to Cade.

"He's practicing. The county fair is coming up and he's entered in the bull riding championship. Don't worry. Pierce knows what he's doing. He's got the touch." Cade paused and looked from Tammy to Ahmed and to the car parked next to his truck. "What are you two doing here?"

"Ahmed found something" was all Tammy could say before she saw Pierce hop over the fence and onto one angry bull.

Pierce pushed down his cowboy hat to make sure it didn't fly off and grabbed the bull rope as he leapt onto the bull. Dr. Francis had given him the okay and it wasn't a moment too soon. He needed to clear his head and this was the best way to do it. Cade pulled a rope from where he stood off to the side and the gate crashed open. The bull leapt forward into the homemade arena.

With one arm up in the air, Pierce gripped the bull with his thighs as the bull tried to buck him off. The amazing thing about bull riding was that 8 seconds seemed a lifetime. Everything moved in slow motion and Pierce let his body take over as his mind tried to calm itself. Tammy wasn't the only thing that kept him awake last night. He also started to remember things, snippets of events. Being in a car, two voices talking to each other, and he remembered saying "I don't know! Stop asking me."

As the hooves pounded the dirt, bits of his memories hung in the air like floating puzzle pieces as he tried to push them together to no avail. A sharp whistle from Cade drew his attention. Tammy was practically crawling over the fence and Ahmed stood behind her. Pierce shifted his hips as he pushed off and leaped from the bull. With the rider off his back, the bull rope slid off and the bull sauntered back to his barn where some fresh treats waited him.

Pierce used his hat to smack the dirt off his jeans as he sauntered over to the fence. "What's going on?"

"Oh, thank God you're okay!" Tammy threw her arms around him, as she stood halfway up the fence.

"Of course I'm okay. Are you okay? Did something happen?" Pierce asked as he was engulfed in a hug.

"I found something. We need to go to your farm. Tammy's already called Henry. He's meeting us out there," Ahmed said before turning away and walking to his car.

Pierce hopped the fence and reached his truck in seconds. He knew better than to ask Ahmed what he had found. He just wanted to hurry to find out what it was.

Pierce pulled into his driveway and felt as if he were leading the Fourth of July parade. Cade must've called the whole family. His parents had hurried down the front steps of their house when he drove by. Behind Cade and his parents were a couple of sheriff's cars, two Mercedes, a family sedan, and a huge Ford truck. Ahead of him, Henry stood with the sunlight reflecting off his suit like a beacon.

Pierce parked his truck and headed straight for where Tammy was standing with Henry and Ahmed. "What did you find?"

Ahmed shot him a glance. It looked like Pierce would have to wait until the whole town got there. Cade and his parents hurried to his side. The whole group formed a circle around them.

"What did you find?" Marcy asked. Pierce looked over at his mother and saw that she had a death grip on his father.

"The fire was started in the kitchen. It looks as if they lit the table where his liquor was sitting. It spread across the kitchen and hallway." Ahmed walked through the remains of the house. The back was completely exposed, but the walls surrounding the living room were still intact.

"Dr. Oldham was found here." Ahmed pointed to a place in the middle of the living room. "Pierce remembers waking up here," he said pointing to a spot closer to the burned hallway. Knowing Pierce was the only suspect, I guessed the police didn't do a detailed search for blood anywhere else in the room."

"They wouldn't have. Cause of death was obvious and blood was plainly visible," Marshall explained.

"Except there was more blood." Pulling out a little ultraviolet light, he made his way over to the brick fireplace. "Pierce, if you don't mind." Ahmed gestured for Pierce to stand by the fireplace. He used the light to scan the wall at Pierce's height.

It only took a second and the group gasped as a small round spot appeared under the light right where Pierce's head would go. "I believe you were knocked unconscious. If you don't think it's too much, I want to reenact what we do know. Please, Cade, lie down where Dr. Oldham was found. Thank you. Marshall, please stand by the fireplace and make sure Pierce doesn't injure himself."

"Why would I injure myself?" Pierce said from where he was standing near Cade who was now lying on the floor moaning theatrically.

"Because of this." Ahmed shoved him hard, driving Pierce across the room toward the fireplace.

Pierce automatically fought back as Ahmed shoved and pushed at him. Suddenly the floating puzzle pieces slammed to earth and crashed down upon him.

"Stop! I remember!" Pierce called out as Ahmed caught his shirt moments before he would have crashed into the fireplace.

"Tell me," Ahmed said quietly.

Pierce was so lost in the memories flying around he didn't hear or see anyone. He was looking down at himself standing in the living room with Dr. Oldham. "There were two of them standing in front of us. We were standing here. Dr. Oldham was on my left. Dr. Oldham pulled out his phone and dialed 9-1-1. The small one reached for the bat I kept next to the sofa. In one swing, Dr. Oldham went down hard. I jumped the little guy, trying to save Dr. Oldham, but the bigger one got to me first. He nailed me with a punch to the face. I stumbled back…" Pierce felt his still slightly swollen eye before continuing.

"I landed a kick to his face, but he landed a harder jab to my ribs. I stumbled backward and with a swift kick to the gut, I practically flew back into the fireplace. The last thing I remember is seeing the bigger man rip the bat from the smaller one and smash the bat down on Dr. Oldham's head. That's when everything went dark."

He felt Tammy's hand slide into his. The feeling brought him out of his trance. His mother was quietly crying into her apron. Mo was holding Dani who was not-so-quietly sobbing into his shoulder. Everyone else stood in shocked silence as if having relived the night with him.

"Pierce," Marshall asked quietly stepping forward. "The blood splatter on Dr. Oldham's shirt that they think is yours. Who's is it? Is there any way it's yours?"

"It's not mine. I never got near Dr. Oldham until after I woke up," Pierce answered.

"Is it Oldham's own blood then?"

"No. It was the man who killed him. It was blood from the broken nose I gave him. It was flowing down his face as he raised the bat…"

"I'm calling the special prosecutor," Henry said as he hurried off with his cell phone in hand.

"I've already dialed Detective Basher," Annie said as she ducked out to return to her cruiser.

Marcy enveloped Pierce in a hug.

"This is great news. What Henry didn't tell you before walking away is that all of this DNA evidence will make it close to impossible to prove you killed Dr. Oldham. The detectives will be forced to clear you as soon as those tests come back in and go after the real killers," Kenna told the crowd as she gave Pierce's shoulder a squeeze.

Pierce smiled in relief as his brothers surrounded him. He hugged them all and felt like crying for a moment before his sisters-in-law got to him.

"Would you like me to release these details to the media? If I do and the perps hear it, then they may come after you." Morgan said.

"Do it. This time I'll be ready for them," Pierce said with clarity he hadn't felt in days.

"Hasn't my apartment been shot up enough?" Paige teased as she hugged her little brother.

"Wait. Before we do anything, we need a plan," Cole said. "We want to decide if we release the statement or if Morgan leaks it. We also need a plan to capture these guys if they come after Pierce again."

"Good idea. Cole, Ahmed, Miles, Cade, why don't you all come over to my house tonight and we'll develop a plan," Marshall said as the men started to step aside to discuss getting together.

The women came to stand next to Tammy with their arms crossed over their chests. Annie narrowed her eyes, "I say we women meet and come up with a better plan."

"You may meet at our house if you'd like," Mo said as the lone male in their group.

"Yes! Please do. We're smart and it's not like most of us don't have experience in this kind of thing. Unfortunately," Dani pointed out.

"Great. Let's see if Marcy can babysit." Annie said as she and Paige walked over to see if her mother would watch the grandbabies for a couple hours.

"Tammy, we'll send a car for you. The others live so much closer and I will feel better having someone drive you home at night if this goes late." Mo gave her a smile and Tammy thanked him. She already had a plan formulating in her mind and she knew without a doubt the men would hate it.

CHAPTER ELEVEN

Pierce grabbed another beer out of Marshall's refrigerator and sat down with the group of men. They'd been talking for an hour already. Cole had come up with a simple plan of surveillance, but then Ahmed tossed in the idea of using Pierce as bait. Suddenly the plan got a lot more complicated. The one being discussed now involved a body double, which sounded cool to Pierce.

At the knock on the door, Marshall's dog, Bob, raised his head from where he was using the vizsla stare to will the bowl of cheese puffs closer and determined it wasn't worth barking at the new arrival. Pierce watched the dog out of the corner of his eye and as soon as everyone turned their attention to the door, Bob shot up and placed his front feet on the table. His head dove into the bowl of cheese puffs and a second later he was resting his head quietly again on the table. The only evidence of his having ever moved was the yellow cheese powder on his nose.

"Hey, guys," Will greeted as he walked in. "Hope you don't mind me stopping by, but Kenna went over to Dani's to hang out so I thought I'd see how you all were making out."

"I guess they're having some kind of girls night while we're all over here. They're probably watching *Steel Magnolias* and crying by now," Marshall shuddered.

Tammy was sitting in her living room waiting for Mo's car to arrive. She felt funny accepting it, but Tammy had learned by working with Dani that Mo's offers were really well-mannered orders. If Tammy had driven herself, one of Mo's men would be in a car right behind her. When Mo first moved to town, she would've taken that action as a power trip. But now she and the rest of the town knew better. He didn't have many friends growing up so the people of Keeneston had become his friends and he looked out for them.

At the sound of the knock at her door, Tammy stood up and straightened her simple cotton dress and slipped on her tan heels. She was probably overdressed, but she just felt wrong walking into the enormous, richly furnished house in jeans. She opened the door and looked at the man standing there in a black suit similar to the one Ahmed wore. But even she could tell it wasn't of the same quality. She'd been sent an underling who desperately wanted to be Ahmed.

"Hi. Are you new to Mo's staff? I don't recognize you," she asked as she looked over his short and rather lanky body. It was clear he was trying his hardest to be more muscular, but she didn't know if it was actual muscles or just many layers of clothing.

"I have just arrived from Rahmi last week. It is a great honor to serve His Royal Highness and his princess," the man said slowly with heavily accented English, a smile never tempting his lips.

"Well, welcome to Keeneston. My name is Tammy Fields." Tammy held out her hand and the man just stared at her. "And, your name is?"

"Nabi Ulmalhamsh Mosteghanemi," he said quickly in his native tongue. Tammy blinked. She had no idea where to even start.

"It's nice to meet you, Nabi," She said with a smile on her face hoping he'd forgive her horrible pronunciation.

"No. My name is Nabi Ulmalhamsh Mosteghanemi." With a quick bow of his head, he then motioned that it was time to leave.

Tammy locked the door and wondered if he'd be insulted if she said, "Hey you." Nabi escorted her to the black Mercedes sedan and opened the door for her. The ride didn't take long, but it gave her a chance to think about her plan. Tammy wondered what the other girls would think of it.

The car came to a stop and Tammy hopped out, much to the aggravation of mini-Ahmed. She climbed the stairs and the door was opened by Mo's butler, who she was pretty sure was also very capable of defending the house all on his own.

"Good evening, Miss Fields," he said formally.

"How are you doing, Umar?" Tammy asked with a smile as she noticed mini-Ahmed glare briefly at the butler.

"I'm doing well. Thank you, Miss Fields. The ladies are in their normal spot. Shall I take you?" He said with a grin. Well, it seemed that Umar was enjoying rankling the new guy.

"No, thanks. I know where it is," Tammy told him as she headed off down the long hall. As she passed her favorite Renoir painting, she could already hear Paige's laughter.

The door was partially opened and Tammy walked into Dani's part of the house. Comfortable upholstered chairs and couches filled the room instead of the elegant, yet uncomfortable antiques that graced some of the formal rooms Dani and Mo used when they had company. Instead of priceless masterpieces hanging on the wall, there were family photos. *Steel Magnolias* was on the large flat-screen television as Julia Roberts appeared.

"We're watching a movie?" Tammy asked.

"Tammy!" Dani cheered. "Grab some dessert and have a seat. When Marshall texted Katelyn asking what she was doing, she said we were picking out a chick flick. We didn't want to lie, and this is our best cover. What guy is going to want a play-by-play of a girly movie?" Dani and the rest of the girls laughed.

"Good point! Have you all started talking about Pierce yet?"

Morgan stood up and grabbed another chocolate truffle. "Not yet, we were waiting for you. We had to find out how Nabi did," she said with an evil grin.

Tammy closed the door and popped a truffle in her mouth. "I think he's a mini-Ahmed. Though much stricter. And he wouldn't let me call him Nabi."

"He is a mini-Ahmed!" Dani said with a chuckle. "He's only twenty-one and has studied in the Academy over in Rahmi. He worships Ahmed. Ahmed's not so amused. So he's learned all about Ahmed's professional side and thinks he has to be a mute badass to be like Ahmed. We're working on him."

"What I want to know is what idea you have for Pierce. I saw your face at the farm and you have an idea," Kenna read correctly.

"Well, everyone is assuming Pierce remembers what these guys look like. However, Pierce has no idea. I'm betting the guys will come up with a plan that will make Pierce the bait. My plan is to make me the bait." Tammy paused as she let it sink in. Was she really prepared to do that? If it meant helping Pierce, then the answer was a quick yes.

"Sneaky," Annie finally said. "Pierce said when they attacked him at his house they were wearing masks, but they had taken them off to drive." She started before Kenna jumped in.

"And Tammy got a good look at them driving…" Everyone turned and looked at her. "Did you actually see them?"

"Yes and no. I saw that the bigger guy was driving and he was definitely a male. Besides that, not really. His hair was short, but not buzz-cut."

"I love it!" Annie laughed. Before they could discuss it further, the door opened and Umar led Bridget inside. She strode confidently in and then paused, looking slightly lost. "Bridget! I'm so glad you came! I hope you all don't mind, but Bridget has lots of experience at this kind of thing."

"Of course not! Welcome! Did you find the place easily enough?" Dani asked as she rose from the chair to put an arm around a suddenly uncomfortable-looking Bridget.

"Yes, I did. But then some kid wanted to search every nook and cranny before the butler got to him."

"Oh, no! Umar, tell mini-Ahmed to come apologize," Dani said on a sigh.

"Mini-Ahmed?" Bridget raised an eyebrow in curiosity.

"Yes. He studied Ahmed in school and thinks he's the end-all of security, which he is. But Nabi hasn't learned how to use his skills while in society yet," Dani explained before turning to her butler. "Umar, can you pronounce his name for me. I still can only get Nabi."

"Nabi Ulmalhamsh Mosteghanemi, Your Highness. And, if you don't mind me saying, I think he learned his lesson."

"Thank you for taking care of that. He needs to realize this is a home, not the royal palace, and people need to be treated kindly," Dani smiled.

"Actually, Miss Springer took care of it."

"I guess I need to be the one apologizing," Bridget said sheepishly. "I might have temporarily disabled him."

"It was well done, ma'am. The cook will be bringing you a special treat shortly." Umar sent her a wink and then stoically closed the door.

"Ah, hazing the new guy. Fun times," Bridget said, relaxing a little more. With a quick flick of her wrist, she pulled her long hair into a ponytail and sat down on the sofa next to Annie. "So, what have I missed?"

Katelyn filled her in quickly and Bridget nodded in approval. "It's a good plan, but you need to find a way to let them know you have the information without being obvious."

"Actually," Morgan spoke up, "I have been thinking about that." With a grin, Morgan told them her idea.

Paige let out a low whistle. "We can't let anything slip on that. You know how the guys are. They'll be furious."

"I know! Won't it be fun?" Annie laughed.

"I think I may be of assistance as well." Everyone jumped and turned around to where Mo was standing by the door that connected to his office. "After you put this into motion, you need help and I'll provide the support for that."

"Thank you, husband, but now we have the second topic to cover. So shoo!" Dani blew Mo a kiss. With an elegant bow, Mo headed back into his office. "Now we got that settled, there's something else involving Pierce we need to talk about."

Tammy felt everyone turn and look at her with innocent little smiles on their faces. "What?"

"So, are you two dating now? I mean, you did go on a date to the café," Kenna said with a smile on her face.

"I don't know. Someone interrupted us when I was trying to find out if there was a relationship or not." Tammy glared at Paige and then laughed to show her friend she wasn't being serious.

"Sorry about that. It's a brother-sister thing." Paige shrugged with a smile.

"I have a confession to make," Tammy said, dropping her voice. The women all leaned closer to her. "If you tell anyone, I will go crazy on all of you! Deal?"

"Deal," the group eagerly agreed.

"You know the advice Henry gave me, to act like the kiss was no big deal?" Tammy paused and took a deep breath. "He was *right*! It worked like a charm."

The girls broke out laughing and Tammy felt as if she were finally part of this special group of women. Sure, she'd been friends with them, but not like this. And this, however you describe it, was special.

"Well then, what's the status? Is Pierce falling at your feet?" Katelyn asked as the girls leaned in once again.

"That's the funny thing. At the café he was flirting so heavy with me, I thought I'd burn up on the spot." The girls all fanned themselves and Tammy grinned. So this was what it was like to have a group of friends instead of working to keep a roof over her head all the time. "But then it all changed."

"I didn't do that, did I?" Paige asked, suddenly worried.

"No. I came over to see him and he said he wanted to watch a movie and talk. What does that mean? One second I'm all confident and feeling like the sexiest woman alive. The next, I'm standing there feeling frumpy and wondering what was wrong with me."

"Nothing is wrong with you!" Paige cried as she hurried over to her.

"You're going to laugh, Bridget, but I was trying to be more like you," Tammy said with an embarrassed grin.

"Me?" Bridget's eyes went wide as she looked around.

"Yeah, you're always so confident and sexy. I wanted to be like that. Do you have a secret?" Tammy laughed as she ducked her head to hide the blush on her cheeks.

"Are you messing with me?" Bridget asked suspiciously as she looked down at her black running pants and top. She only had two types of clothes, sporty and military. Not exactly sexy.

"Well, it sounds as if we need to have an intervention for you both!" Paige clapped her hands; Kenna, Dani, and Katelyn squealed; and Annie cringed. "And it all starts with underwear."

"What?" Tammy and Bridget said at the same time.

"Soft, sexy, and silky is key. It gives you a whole new boost of confidence to know you're wearing a sexy little number beneath your clothes," Katelyn explained.

"And I happen to have a whole box in my car! I just got them in and was getting ready to take them over to the shop. I was planning to turn the backroom into a Sugar and Spice room." Paige clapped her hands and hurried out of the room on her mission.

"This gives a whole new meaning to trunk show," Kenna laughed.

"Who knows, maybe it'll distract him from noticing I don't exactly have ample, well, anything," Tammy sighed.

"I guarantee you, Pierce won't find one thing the matter with you. He'll be too busy thanking his lucky stars he finally got you undressed." Morgan shot her a grin and Tammy started thinking this could possibly work.

"Now that that's settled, let's solve this case!" Annie sat back in her chair, popped a truffle in her mouth, and grinned.

"And win a man's heart!" Dani cheered.

Tammy laughed as she and Bridget joked about the pink bags they were carrying with dainty little numbers in them, all thanks to Paige. Mini-Ahmed stood holding the door for Tammy and eyeing Bridget suspiciously.

"What did you do to him?" Tammy whispered.

"Nothing I can't teach you. I'll come over in the afternoon and show you a few moves if you'd like." Bridget paused and took in the shadows of the farm. "I'm actually starting to really like this place. I was supposed to be here only for a week, but I think I'll stay here another week. I've raised Marko since he was a puppy, and I'm finding it hard to give him up. Also, the quietness of the town is really nice."

"Except for the whole murder, fire thing," Tammy sarcastically remarked.

"Hell of a lot better than being shot at all the time. I'll see you tomorrow?"

"True. Tomorrow at three would be perfect." Tammy said good-bye to Bridget and was getting into the Mercedes when Paige called out to her.

"Tammy! I'm glad I caught you before you left. We're having dinner at my parents' house tomorrow. Why don't you join us? I'm sure Mom will want to thank you for all you've done."

"Are you sure? Isn't it a family dinner?" Tammy started to grow a little nervous.

Paige sent her a funny look. "Yeah. And you just spent hours here with half the family. It's not as if you don't know us all, silly."

"But, what about Pierce?" Tammy worried.

"What about him? I'm inviting you and you're coming. See you at six!" Paige gave a little wave and then hopped in her car, effectively ending Tammy's ability to say no thanks. Sure, dinner at the Davies farm. Nothing to be worried about, right?

CHAPTER TWELVE

Tammy pulled her car to a stop outside the crowded farmhouse. She was tired and sore from Bridget's afternoon lesson. Although, she had to admit the combination of knowing how to protect herself and the silk panties she was wearing under her pale yellow sundress did give her a whole new level of confidence.

As she hurried toward the house, she saw Henry's car and suddenly she was able to relax. It must be a working dinner. Phew, she had thought Paige might be setting her up and she didn't want Pierce to think she was pushing a relationship. Nope, she wanted him to prove himself. Her days of jumping him were over—unless they were both naked.

Tammy climbed the steps to the door, but Marcy opened it with a smile before she could knock. "There's the girl who's been working so hard. Come in, come in, I made fried chicken and cheese biscuits. You're just in time!" Marcy grabbed her hand and led her into the chaos.

Little Ryan and Sophie were pressing every musical toy they had, the men were congregated in a circle in animated discussion, and the women were sitting on the couch with their heads pressed together. However, it was Pierce who drew her attention immediately. He stood with his brothers, but she didn't even see them. He looked so handsome in his black slacks and light blue oxford, which outlined his tall frame. Henry had to say her name twice before Tammy heard him.

"Tammy! I was just telling Pierce about the case law that you were able to find in relation to memory loss as a defense and how we can use that in case the rest of his memory doesn't come back and the special prosecutor decides to go forward with the case." Tammy smiled politely as she walked over to their group.

"Thank you, Tammy. I don't think I can tell you what all your hard work means to me." Pierce looked at her in such a way and Tammy seriously reconsidered the whole no-jumping rule she had just sworn off.

Marcy clapped her hands and instantly everyone quieted down, even the babies. "Dinner is ready!"

Paige and Annie scooped up their kids and set them in high chairs around the massive, country-style dining table. The family sat in their regular seats and Tammy waited to see which spot was left. She snagged an empty one and so did Henry. As everyone settled in, the noise died down and all eyes focused on the empty place setting next to Pierce.

Pierce looked at his mother's fine china sitting empty next to him and cringed. Every man at the table knew what that meant. His mother was attempting to set him up. "Ma?"

"Yes, dear?" Marcy smiled innocently and the knot in Pierce's stomach tightened.

"Why is there an empty plate next to me?" Pierce asked just as innocently, even as his heart started to race with anxiety.

"Oh! That? I'm expecting another guest. But, she won't be able to make it until dessert." Marcy took another delicate bite of her dinner and smiled as her sons all looked in terror at the empty plate.

"Ma? Who did you invite to dinner?" Miles asked slowly.

"This nice girl I met at Pierce's arraignment. She's from Keeneston. She was even a cheerleader and is part of the Belles. She just moved back to Lexington and hasn't been able to spend much time in Keeneston yet."

"Don't you think this is poorly timed, Ma?" Cade asked as he glanced between Tammy's head buried in her plate and the way Pierce's face was starting to turn red.

"There is never a poor time for love, dear," Marcy said as she spread some butter on her cheese biscuit.

"Well, I have an exciting announcement." Pierce smiled, even if it was a little overkill. "Tammy and I had a wonderful date the other night. Something I hope we can repeat very soon." He shot her a wide grin and watched as Tammy turned bright red.

"That's wonderful! It's just a shame you haven't asked her yet," Marcy smiled pleasantly.

"So, Tammy, what is it about my little brother you find irresistible?" Marshall asked with an evil twinkle in his eye. Katelyn coughed politely into her napkin and then kicked Marshall under the table.

"I don't understand why you'd wait around for him." Cade shrugged. "What makes him so worth it? Ow!" Cade shot a look to Annie who sat calmly next to him. She slowly placed her fork back on the table.

"Well, it's true." Miles said in his dismissive tone. "Tammy, don't you know you're too good for him?" This time he sent her a wink and Pierce felt like banging his head against the table. This was payback.

"Um, well. I..." Tammy stammered.

Pierce couldn't stand to see Tammy so flustered. The woman who had been his rock was sinking as his brothers interrogated her. "Okay! That's enough. Tammy, just ignore them."

Everyone at the table froze when the doorbell rang. Pierce began to sweat as his mother went to answer the door. First his mom invites another girl to dinner, then his brothers interrogate Tammy, and now she was going to have to sit here and watch a stranger flirt with him because his mom told some random single girl that she had a son desperate to marry. If his mom were really laying it on, then she'd tell this helpless victim that she taught her sons how to do laundry and cook. She probably left out that whole murder charge though. All he knew was that by the end of this night, there would be little chance of Tammy agreeing to another date.

The voices grew nearer and Pierce kept his eyes locked on Tammy. He wouldn't go along with his mother's matchmaking shenanigans while the woman who had found a place in his heart was sitting across the table from him. Tammy looked torn between embarrassment and anger. He'd vote for anger. That was what he was feeling anyway.

"Everyone!" Marcy clapped. They all had their eyes focused squarely on the door to the dining room. "This is Neely Grace Sinclair. You know Martha at the D.A.'s office? This is her granddaughter."

Pierce watched as Tammy's eyes widened and she lowered them to her plate in defeat. What had this woman done with just one look? Pierce chanced a glimpse and almost groaned. She was a knockout. Neely Grace was tall with long chestnut brown hair in shining waves over her shoulders that stopped at her perfectly rounded breasts. She was dressed to perfection in a pair of black slacks and an almost sheer sleeveless white silk blouse. Two weeks ago, Pierce would have scooped his mom up and kissed her for bringing Neely Grace to dinner. But not now. Not as Tammy looked like someone had just kicked her dog. Pierce tried to get Tammy's attention, but she refused to look at him.

"Neely Grace just moved back from Washington, D.C. She finished up a clerkship with our senator! Isn't that fascinating? Now she's an associate attorney in Lexington. Neely dear, do you remember Pierce from high school?"

Pierce thought back to high school and remembered what his mother had said about Neely Grace being a cheerleader.

"I think so. You weren't in my class, though, were you?" Pierce asked reluctantly.

Neely Grace smiled and Tammy tossed her napkin to the table. Henry preened next to her as she answered, "No, I wasn't. I was in between you and Paige. It's nice to see you again, though. I'm sorry for the trouble you're going through. Anyone who remembers you would know you'd never harm anyone," she said with a perfect tone she inherited from the Belles and perfected on the Hill. "Paige! I remember you, too. It's so nice to see you after all these years. Congratulations on your marriage and the addition to your family."

Oh, she was smooth. A born and bred Belle—the original version, not the new model like Jasmine. When Neely Grace left for college, the Belles were perfection in speech, manners, and grace.

"Let me introduce you!" Marcy started at the head of the table with his dad and worked her way around to Pierce and then across the table to Tammy. But then Tammy surprised him. She held her head high and introduced herself.

"I don't suppose you remember me. I wasn't part of the same circles as you traveled in."

Neely Grace cocked her head to the side and looked hard at Tammy. "Trailer Park Tammy," she whispered. Tammy refused to cower and held her gaze. "Kids can be so cruel. I hope I never did anything hurtful to you. But if I did, I am so very sorry. I always remember you as the nicest girl. You always had a smile on your face and believe it or not, that's what I remember the most about you."

"Thank you. You were never mean to my face and I guess that's about all I can say. Before she left, my mother taught me to treat others with respect and manners. Something the Belles should have learned."

Pierce wanted to pump his fist in the air and leap across the table to plant a kiss on Tammy's lips. She was beautiful in her confidence. She may be a good six inches shorter than Neely Grace, but right now she was the most regal woman he'd ever seen.

"I couldn't agree with you more. It's one of the reasons I haven't been back to Keeneston much. The Belles have already reached out to invite me back into their fold, but Jasmine was a snob in high school and I fear it's only gotten worse."

Tammy gave a little nod and then returned Neely Grace's smile. Just like that, a peace agreement was made between them.

"And this is the man I was telling you about, Henry Rooney," Marcy said with a huge grin on her face. Mouths dropped, including Henry's, as Pierce stared at his mother. She had played him. She had played them all.

Tammy snickered, Morgan snorted, Katelyn politely hid her laugh behind a cough, and Annie let out a belly laugh. Soon the whole table was full of laughter. Pierce stood up and grabbed the clean china next to him. "Sweetheart, why don't you come sit by me and Neely Grace and Henry can get to know each other better," Pierce said with a grin made large with laughter and relief.

Tammy hurried around the table and settled in next to Pierce. Something in their relationship had just shifted. She felt it. As he rested his hand on her thigh underneath the tablecloth, she felt his heat burn through her skirt. He had just claimed her as his in front of his whole family, if she'd have him. Who was she kidding! She'd have him even if his fingers weren't dancing lightly up her inner thigh making her thoughts completely muddled.

Henry cleared his throat and checked Neely Grace out as she sat down next to him. He looked like a cat that had just caught a mouse. "Mmm, if being sexy was a crime, you'd be guilty as charged." Henry smirked as he checked her out.

Tammy whispered a curse word and shook her head as Neely Grace just smiled at Henry as if he were a little boy. "Don't you think you should've led with, 'Is there an airport nearby because my heart just took off?'"

"With lines like that I could love you beyond a reasonable doubt," Henry said with a cockiness that he used in court. And, it usually worked on women. Henry was pretty attractive when he wasn't being a goober.

"If loving you is a crime, then I'm in for a life sentence," Neely Grace sweetly joked back to him.

"This is like watching a bizarre, 'You've Been Served' dance-off, but with pick-up lines," Pierce whispered in Tammy's ear before placing a quick kiss right behind her ear, causing her to shiver with excitement.

Henry sneezed and then looked up at her with smoldering eyes. "I sneezed because God blessed me with you."

"Apart from being sexy, what do you do for a living?" Neely Grace asked with an innocent smile.

"I'm a lawyer. Wanna take a look at my briefs?"

"Is that all you got, hot stuff?" Neely Grace asked him with a wink.

"Nice shoes, want to f…"

"I'm so glad you all have so many things in common!" Marcy interrupted. "Morgan, dear, when are you and Miles going on your honeymoon?"

Miles cleared his throat in an attempt to stop laughing before answered his mother. "We'll go as soon as all the charges have been dropped."

"Thank you all. I'm so grateful for everything you've done for me. I just wish Cy were here," Pierce sighed and felt bad for even saying anything about Cy.

"Who's Cy? Wait, you mean your older brother? Where is he?" Neely Grace asked as she looked around at the quite table.

"He's overseas for work at the moment," Miles responded politely before turning to Pierce. "You know he'd be here in a heartbeat if you needed him to be," Miles said gently.

"I know. I've talked to him a couple of times and he's told me. I shouldn't have said anything. I just miss him."

"I hope to have all the charges dismissed against you before he could ever get home," Henry said reassuringly.

Tammy felt her stomach plummet as Pierce's attention drifted away from her again—just as it did the other night at his apartment. Instead of turning to her for support, he turned away. Tammy's leg was nudged and she turned to look at Paige. Paige's eyes were wide as she tried to gesture quietly to start plan "B".

After the women had talked about catching the bad guys and before looking over lingerie, they had come up with a plan to catch Pierce's attention and hold it.

"Now is *so* not the time," Tammy whispered. "He's upset."

"It's the perfect time. It'll take his mind off of it." Paige shot her a quick smile. "Well! Thanks for dinner, Ma. It was wonderful as always. Annie, should we take the children into the living room to play?"

"Oh! Can I come, too? I'd love a little girl talk. Tammy, would you care to join us?" Katelyn asked as she stood up.

"What a wonderful idea!" Marcy clasped her hands together and looked at the table. "Well, boys, why don't you clean up while we chat. Neely Grace, maybe if we ask nicely enough, Tammy will tell us all about that incredibly gorgeous man she brought to the wedding." Marcy gracefully arose from the table with Neely Grace and followed the women into the living room. Annie hid a laugh in the baby blanket as she lifted Sophie out of the high chair.

"Jeez, Paige, did you have to tell your mom?" Tammy asked mortified at what was unfolding in front of her.

"I didn't!"

Marcy and Neely Grace joined them in the living room. She met their shocked faces with a large smile on her face. "Oh please, I'm a mother of six. I know everything. Now sit back and learn." Marcy shot them a sly grin and then gasped. She tapped Tammy's arm and laughed, "Oh, how positively wicked! Well, when in Greece, right?" Marcy tittered.

"What is this about?" Neely Grace asked as she turned her back to the men all staring at them to lean in closer to the tight group of women gossiping.

"Men, dear. See, Tammy here has been in love with my son for two years." Tammy thought she'd burst into flames at the mortification of this conversation. "And my son has been too dumb to realize a good thing right in front of his face. For two years, he's been fluttering around with, frankly, bimbos. Tonight I'm putting a stop to it."

"You? We're putting a stop to it," Katelyn whispered while she kept a smile on her face.

"Well, watch and learn, ladies. It's not as if I went up to Jake and put some of my fried chicken in front of him to win him over. Nope, forty years ago he was the catch of the town. I haven't forgotten all my mama taught me," Marcy winked.

"And you're hooking me up with Henry as a distraction?" Neely Grace asked with slight confusion in her perfectly smooth Southern voice.

"Oh, that was just a perk. No, I think you're great for each other. Henry is like a puppy dog. He just needs someone with a firm hand on the leash to train him to be the perfect husband. I bet you find a loyal and loving man as soon as you break through that unfortunate exterior."

"For some reason, I believe you. You were always nice to me, even if my mom didn't like you after you left the Belles. Although, I don't even like my mom much, hence, why I live in Lexington," Neely Grace said sadly. "Well, it's not like I can just go home with him. That would stroke his ego and I don't know any other way to get to know him better." The change of subject gave a clear indication she didn't want to talk about the past.

"As I said, leave it to me." With a wink, Marcy straightened up and gasped, "Neely Grace! That's horrible. Cars these days, they just don't run like they used to. You shouldn't be driving in the dark with the battery acting up. Maybe Annie and Cade can give you a ride home?" Marcy looked pointedly at Annie.

"Oh! Normally we'd love to, but it's Sophie's bedtime and I don't know how comfortable you'd be in the backseat with a car seat digging into you," Annie said apologetically.

Henry stepped forward from the crowd of men. "I can take her home. I'm, um, heading to Lexington anyway to go to the office store."

"Oh! That would be perfect. Thank you for being such a gentleman, Henry." Marcy smiled at him and then turned back to the group.

"See, men are so easy. Tammy, dear," she said more loudly this time, "did you put that new deadbolt on your door yet?"

"Well, no. Do I need one?" Tammy asked with real confusion.

"Certainly! With all this horrid stuff going on, I can't stand the thought of you at your apartment all alone with only a flimsy lock to keep you safe." Marcy looked affronted by the question.

Pierce strode into the room, looking worried. "You don't have a lock on your door?"

"Sure I do, it's in the knob. I don't need anything more." Tammy suddenly felt defensive about her poor door.

"Sure you do." Pierce turned to his mother and squeezed her shoulder gently, "Don't worry, Ma. I'll follow Tammy home and put in a deadbolt tonight. I'll make sure she's safe." Tammy almost melted on the spot at the sizzling protective look in his eyes.

"Oh, thank you! I'll rest a lot easier now." Marcy patted Pierce's hand as Pierce turned to say good-bye to the men.

Marcy winked at the room full of girls. "And, ladies, that is how it's done."

CHAPTER THIRTEEN

Tammy looked in the mirror of her tiny bathroom and pushed up her breasts. Okay, she could do this. She was a sexy siren. She applied the red lip gloss and rolled her skirt once to show more leg. As she came out of the bathroom, she eyed Pierce with a drill as he made a hole for the deadbolt.

Tammy sat on the couch and waited while he worked. Maybe it wasn't sexy just sitting there? She crossed her legs and arched back against the couch. No, she just looked like she threw out her back. She leaned over and used her arms to push up her breasts. Nope, now she just looked cold. Maybe if she sat at the edge of the couch and crossed her legs and shifted, *thunk*! She fell with a complete lack of grace and landed on the floor. She scrambled up just as Pierce turned off the drill and slid the deadbolt into place.

It was no use. She was not sexy. Pierce moved quickly as he tightened the screws and tested out the new bolt. Happy with his work, he stood up and dusted off his pants. "All done."

"Thank you. I really appreciate it," Tammy smiled, but she was just hoping he'd hurry up and leave. She was failing miserably at this sexy thing. The fancy panties weren't even helping.

"Tammy, there's something I have been meaning to talk to you about." Pierce looked a little nervous as he started talking to her. "I know I have been running hot and cold, but it's not because of you."

Tammy's heart sank even lower than it was already. He was breaking up with her before they even started dating. Worse, he was using the "it's not you, it's me" line. How depressing is that? "Of course not. Well, thanks for telling me and for installing the deadbolt. Good-bye, Pierce."

"Good-bye?" Pierce reached out and grabbed her arms and brought her lithe figure against his. "Tammy, I'm trying to tell you that the reason is because I care for you and, quite frankly, I just don't know how to handle it. If it were up to me, I'd just kiss you and let my feelings speak for themselves. But I'm afraid I might scare you away. You've been waiting two years and you deserve something special."

"Oh, Pierce! Shut up and kiss me!" Tammy smiled as her heart pounded.

Pierce returned her smile. "Yes, ma'am." He bent down slowly as Tammy raised her chin to meet his lips. They were soft and gentle as he brushed them against hers. Slowly he applied more pressure, his hands wrapping around her and holding her loosely as he deepened the kiss.

Tammy felt the kiss down to her toes. Her body tingled and she leaned against him. The hardness of his body excited her more. Pierce bent down and picked her up in a swift move. His lips never left hers as he carried her into the bedroom. He placed her gently on the small double bed and stood between her legs looking down at her. Tammy bit her lip gently as she unbuttoned his shirt and praised herself for not just ripping it off. When his shirt dropped to the floor, he leaned over her and placed a kiss on her lips as he worked her skirt over her hips.

Tammy ran her hands over his bare chest. She explored its ripples and expanse, before lifting her arms over her head so that he could slowly pull off her top before dropping it blindly to the ground.

"If I had known you were wearing these under your clothes, I would have stripped you down long ago," Pierce growled as he stalked her onto the bed. "But now it's time to take them off."

* * *

Pierce grinned and sent a wink to Tammy as he leapt onto the bull. The buzzer sounded, the gate opened, and Pierce held on with all he had as the bull tried to throw him to the ground.

Pierce had woken Tammy up early that morning and driven her to the Keeneston County Fair to watch him compete in the bull-riding contest. He had loved showing her off to his friends and competitors. They had their bleach-blonde groupies and he had the real deal.

The buzzer sounded again and Pierce leapt off as the clowns raced out to herd the bull away from where he landed. He had stayed on for the full 8 seconds and had moved up to first on the leaders' board when the judges' scores were revealed. Damn, it was a great day. A win and the girl—it couldn't get any better.

"You did great!" Tammy squealed as she jumped into his arms.

"Thanks. Now, I want to go show you off for a bit. Some of the guys and their gals want to check out the rest of the fair. Are you up to it?"

"Sure!" Tammy said excitedly. She loved fairs. She was the master at all games. When she was growing up, she went to the fair every day for a week to avoid being at home.

"Great. Let me show you how to win at these games. Maybe I'll even win you a bear." Pierce slung his arm over her shoulder and led her over to the waiting group of friends.

Tammy and Pierce teased each other as they made their way through the fair. All the men enjoyed showing their dates how to hold the water gun or how to throw the dart. The girls tittered away and pouted when they lost. Tammy, however, just smiled and quietly won game after game.

"Oh! Ring toss! Let's see if I can win!" one of the women called out as she dragged her date with her.

"I guess I don't need to teach you to play this. I wouldn't mind winning one of our matches," Pierce laughed as he juggled the huge teddy bear, cotton candy, and a stuffed horse that was big enough for his niece or nephew to ride.

"Well, ring toss is my worst game," Tammy teased.

Pierce set down her winnings and pulled her back against his chest as they stood watching the others play first. He bent his head and placed a kiss on the curve of her neck as he squeezed her hips with his hands. "Let's put a wager on this round, you up for it?"

"Of course. What should we wager?" Tammy asked on a heavy breath.

"If I win, I get to find out which sexy undergarments you're wearing under those tight jeans that are tormenting me. And if you win, I'll give you a very sensual massage and pleasure every inch of you." Pierce whispered in her ear before nipping gently on her lobe. Tammy felt the shiver go down her back as his lips trailed down her neck. "Looks like it's our turn. Ladies first."

Tammy looked at the ring and tried to decide which was better. They both seemed to be a win for her. As she tossed the ring and it rattled over the bottle, she grinned. She could never lose on purpose, even if it was to Pierce.

Pierce gave a very satisfied grin as he grabbed the pink stuffed unicorn she had just won. "Well, let's get back to your apartment. I have a bet I'm eager to fulfill."

Tammy woke to the ringing of her phone early the next morning. She would've answered it if she didn't have a large masculine arm wrapped tightly around her. It was a pretty easy decision: lying naked in bed with Pierce or answering the phone at this ungodly hour. The phone silenced and Tammy wiggled her bottom against Pierce, eliciting a groan and a kiss on the neck. Now this was a way to wake up.

Tammy slid her hand down his leg and the phone rang again. "Don't you think you should get the phone?" Pierce whispered into her ear as his hands cupped her breasts.

"Not particularly," she panted as the blasted phone rang again and again.

"I think you should. It could be important."

"Fine," she signed as she picked up the phone.

"Tammy, get up. We need to find Pierce and get to the Lexington Police Station immediately. Do you have any idea where he is?" Henry barked into the phone.

Pierce rolled her nipple between his fingers. "Mmm, he's staying above Southern Charms."

"He's not there and we need to find him!"

"Maybe he's exercising. I'm sure I can find him. I'll head out and look for him and then meet you at the office," Tammy said as she tried to control her breathing.

"Hurry!" Henry yelled a second before the line went dead.

Pierce ran a hand over her hip and Tammy smacked him. "I have to find you. The police want to talk to you." Pierce nibbled his way down her neck and rolled her over. He used his knee to spread her legs as he settled over her.

Tammy looked up into his face and smiled. "We need to get going," Tammy said half-heartedly.

"I'm supposed to be exercising. I should be hot and sweaty when you find me and bring me in. You wouldn't want me to lie, would you?" Pierce bent his arms and leaned down to give her a searing kiss to end all discussion.

Pierce opened the door to Henry's office and followed Tammy inside. He couldn't get this silly little grin off his face. Pierce was thinking of their morning and wasn't paying attention when he ran into Tammy. Looking up, he saw why she had stopped in her tracts. His whole family, Kenna, Will, Dani, Mo, Ahmed, and Bridget stood in the office waiting for them.

Every pair of eyes went from him to Tammy and back again. Cade snickered and Annie smacked him before Mo elegantly cleared his throat and stepped forward. "We all wanted to be here to show our support of your innocence. Besides," he shrugged smoothly, "I might already have a public apology in the works providing the evidence comes back as we think it will."

Ahmed gave Pierce and the rest of the guys a slight nod to his head before Morgan spoke up. "And I'm ready with a statement for the media as soon as the charges have been dropped," she said, winking to the girls.

Marshall slapped Pierce on the back. "Annie, Bridget, and the guys have been doing our own investigation. We don't have any leads to give them yet, but we do have a lot of names to cross off the suspect list."

"I have a feeling you'll get more leads soon," Morgan said with confidence as she straightened her suit coat. "Let's go clear your name."

Pierce sat quietly between Henry and Tammy as the detectives read the DNA report. "Well, it appears your memory was correct. The evidence shows the blood wasn't yours." Detective Basher tossed the folder onto the table. "It looks like we owe you an apology. Surely you understand we were just doing our job."

"Was it your job to parade me past the television cameras and give damning press conferences, Detective Cowell?" Pierce said with contempt.

"The public has a right to know, Mr. Davies."

"And so they shall. Detective Cowell will be giving a press conference shortly declaring your innocence and apologizing for any hardship to you and your family," Basher told Pierce.

"I will not!"

"It's a direct order from the mayor, Cowell. The governor of our Commonwealth called and personally demanded it. You're doing it," Basher said forcefully.

"I'm glad someone has the decency to do the right thing," Henry gave a slight nod to Basher. "Do you have any other leads?"

"None. But we do have the killer's DNA and are running it through every database we can to try to find a match. Sheriff Davies also handed over the notes on his investigation, which I'll go through right after our press conference. I'm not giving up, Mr. Davies. I will find out who did this," Basher promised.

"Thank you," Pierce said. "And, Detective Basher, I know you were just doing your job."

Basher gave him a quick nod before ending the conference. "Let's meet the others in the conference room and go down to the press conference. The sooner we get it over with, the sooner I can get back to investigating the case." Basher stood up and opened the door to the interview room. Pierce clasped Tammy's hand in his. Now he felt he could give himself fully to her with the cloud of the trial no longer handing over him.

"Now, do you remember what I told you to say?" Miles asked Morgan for the fifth time as the family walked down the stairs and out the front door of the police station.

"Yes, husband," Morgan whispered as Detective Cowell started the press conference. He spoke of the DNA evidence proving Pierce's innocence and apologized for any hardships to him and his family. He further told the crowd that he'd find the guilty party and bring them to justice. Morgan fought the urge to roll her eyes and then finally stepped forward to speak after being introduced by Cowell.

"Hello. My name is Morgan Davies and I have a prepared statement to make on behalf of Pierce Davies and his family. After, there will be no questions. We've all known Pierce was innocent and the trials he and his family have gone through have been great. We appreciate the love and support from all of our friends and neighbors.

"Mr. Davies was framed, but justice will prevail now that his innocence has been proven and Ms. Fields has come forward as an eye witness who is able to identify the perpetrators."

Tammy felt Pierce's hand tighten on hers as he looked down at her with narrowed eyes. She smiled serenely and tried not to worry about the angry looks she was receiving from every man there.

"Ms. Fields will be meeting with police in the near future to assist with identifying the criminals and to help originate new leads, but for now the Davies family and Ms. Fields ask for privacy as they put this nightmare behind them. Thank you," Morgan concluded.

The group turned around quietly, ignoring the questions being hurled at them by the media, and retreated to the conference room at the police station. The women instinctively moved together to stand their ground.

"What?" Kenna asked the glaring men innocently.

"*Steel Magnolias*, huh?" Marshall asked with his hands on his hips.

"I swear, if you weren't the mother of my child and the love of my life…" Cole snapped at Paige. "What in the hell were you thinking?"

"Very well put," Will said crossing his arms and staring at Kenna.

The ladies simply held their ground, refusing to be intimidated. Pierce paced back and forth quietly for a moment and then erupted. "Do you know what you've done?" His face had turned red and Tammy suddenly felt a little sick to her stomach. "You just put Tammy's life in danger! These men will find her and kill her to keep her quiet!"

"I know," Tammy whispered.

"You know? I can't believe you let them talk you into this!"

"They didn't. It was my idea." Tammy found her voice and raised it to defend the others who supported her in her plan.

"Your idea? Why would you do this?" Pierce asked confused.

"Because I love you, why do you think? I'd do anything to prevent seeing you hurt again. Even ruining your grand plan for glory by sacrificing yourself to catch these guys," Tammy shot back.

"So, that's why you think I'm upset? Because you stole my thunder?"

"We all know you Davies men hate not getting your way, so yeah, I do."

"Then you know that I take great pleasure in saying this: You're wrong, Tammy. The reason I'm so upset is because I love you more than my own life. You are my world now. How could you not know that after last night?"

Tammy felt her heart constrict and tears start to flow down her cheeks. She laughed when she heard a nose being blown.

"Sorry, but that was just so sweet!" Dani cried into Mo's silk handkerchief.

"Come on!" Marcy clapped as her eyes shimmered, "let's head out to the farm and figure out how to deal with this together." Marcy shooed everyone out of the room to leave Tammy and Pierce alone.

Pierce wrapped her up in her arms and looked into her eyes. "We'll handle this together because we're an unbeatable team. Deal?" Tammy nodded when she couldn't find the words. "Good. Now are you going to be this quiet every time I tell you how much I love you?"

"No, and I promise to always tell you that I love you, too." Tammy rose up on her tiptoes and sealed the promise with a kiss. "Now, let's get to work so that we can move on with our lives together."

CHAPTER FOURTEEN

Pierce rubbed his head as he listened to the debate flying around the room. Everyone had an idea on how to protect Tammy. She sat quietly by his side and he found it so hard to focus on the task at hand when all he wanted to do was make love to her again. She had cast a fairy spell over him and being forced to sit there with her body pressed against his side was torturing him.

"Okay, enough!" Pierce paused when he realized he said it so loudly. "Ahmed, Marshall, what is the game plan?"

Ahmed began, "At all times, there will be at least one, but most likely two of my men watching Tammy. Now my dear, do not worry if they are out of sight. That is the point. Just feel confident knowing that they are there."

"And one of my deputies will be in plainclothes as well," Marshall told them.

"Also, I want you to take Marko. Tammy, do you remember the commands I showed you the other day?" Bridget smiled as Tammy nodded. "Marko won't let anything happen to you. And neither will I."

"Thank you, Bridget," Tammy stood and hugged her new friend. She was heartbroken that Bridget was leaving next week for the Middle East.

"I'll also be with her the whole time," Pierce said as he laced his fingers through hers.

"Well, that settles that!" Marcy beamed. "Thank you all for all your help. I have lunch ready. Ahmed, please call your men in to eat. I know they're out there somewhere in the fields nearby. I can't have you all going on a stakeout hungry."

Tammy tried to focus on her work, but it was hard with Pierce sitting across the room from her. She was at the end of her rope. Ever since this morning when he declared his love for her, Confident Tammy wanted to leap on him, literally. But they were never given the chance. After Marcy's lunch, Henry asked her to come back to the office to help with the cases that were piling up.

The phone had been ringing off the hook with mysterious sightings of strangers in town. Somehow John Wolfe had found out every word of the plan and soon after the whole town was calling nonstop. They were either warning of people they didn't know or offering to help with personal protection. Old man Tabernacle even offered up a guard pig to lie against the door. He swore no human force would be able to get past his pig.

"Okay, that's it!" Tammy cried as she hung up the phone. "I can't take it anymore. It's time for dinner and I have a frozen pizza calling my name at home."

"I need to stop by Paige's apartment and pick up my clothes and Gus. I'll run and do that while Henry's here and you can give Bridget a call. She wanted to drop Marko off at night. Henry, I'm going out for a bit!" Pierce yelled into the back of the office.

"Gotcha covered for the next thirty minutes. Then I have myself a hot date." Henry strutted out and posed as he flexed his biceps. "Some lucky lady has two tickets to the gun show tonight."

"I'll be back in ten and I don't even know what to say about that." Pierce shook his head and walked out as Henry holstered his guns.

"Bless your heart, Henry, but you can be the biggest goober," Tammy said flatly. "I've had about all I can take." Tammy rose from her seat and went over to Henry. "First, the shiny suits have to go."

"What? These are awesome," Henry defended.

"No, they're 1990s mob wanna-be outfits. Take off your coat and tie, and then unbutton the top button to your dress shirt." Tammy tapped her foot as Henry pouted and slowly did what he was told. "Great. Now roll up your sleeves."

"There. Is this better?" Henry did a slow turn and Tammy nodded in satisfaction. Gone was the sleazy attorney act and in his place was a downright attractive man.

"Yes. Now, I listened to you about Pierce and it worked, right? So now you need to listen to me. I take it this date is with Neely Grace?"

"That's right. I got a Grade A Premium date."

Tammy sighed a long-suffering groan and shook her head. "Nooo! For all the years I have been with you, I've been telling you that women don't want to be treated as cows or any other kind of animal. We don't like pick-up lines. We don't like being hit on. We like being talked to like normal human beings."

"Fine. I'll give it a shot, but I don't think it'll work."

The door opened as Bridget and Marko walked in. Bridget looked amused as she came into the office. "It's not every day you see a man walking down the street pushing a bird cage."

Tammy picked up her purse and gave Marko a pat. "Try it, Henry. I like the new Neely Grace. So be chivalrous, kind, and listen to what she has to say."

"And no pick-up lines!" Bridget and Tammy shouted before the door closed.

Tammy, Bridget, and Marko made it to the front of the Blossom Café sooner than Tammy would have liked. She was really enjoying learning more about Bridget. They were about to turn down the street toward the back of the café when they heard the screaming.

"What's that?" Bridget asked as she picked up speed.

"I think it's Miss Daisy." Tammy rounded the corner and froze in fright. Miss Daisy, Miss Violet, and Miss Lily stood blocking the bottom of the stairs. Pierce was holding a bag and Gus sat on his shoulder. Miss Violet was tapping her wooden spoon against the palm of her hand, taunting Pierce as if she were preparing for a fight. Miss Lily was being subtler as she moved her broom out from behind her and placed it at her side.

"What is this, the Granny Gang?" Bridget asked sarcastically.

"Worse, much worse!" Tammy hurried forward, but it was too late.

"What do you mean I can't go upstairs? I'm staying here to protect her," Pierce's raised voice reached her.

"That's not all your doing, young man, and there's no hanky-panky going on in my apartment!" Miss Daisy stepped forward and smacked his hand with her kitchen towel.

"That's so archaic! It doesn't matter what Tammy and I do. We're grown-ups, for crying out loud." Pierce's posture changed as he tried to angle past the granny wall.

"I don't think so, young man!" Miss Lily brought the broom down on the shoulder not occupied by a bird. Gus jumped over Pierce's head and landed on the broom, biting the straw bristles. Miss Lily screamed and waved the broom in the air, trying to dislodge Gus.

Miss Lily's screams left off as Gus's shrieks of delight at this new game picked up. He clung onto the broom with everything he had as Miss Lily ran in a circle shaking the broom as her sisters chased after her. Gus flew off the broom and snatched Miss Violet's spoon out of the air.

"Gus! Get back here! Drop it," Pierce called as he tried to snatch the bird out of the air. Gus flew high into the air and then dive-bombed the group. The women screeched, Pierce cursed, and Gus laughed as he finally found a place to land… right on Miss Daisy's head.

Everyone froze. Gus took the wooden spoon out of his mouth and held it in a claw. "Aw, that's a good bird!"

Miss Daisy's eyes were wide and wild as Miss Lily crept forward. "Don't move, Daisy Mae." Slowly, she raised the broom into the air…

"No!" Miss Daisy cried, but it was too late. Miss Lily brought the broom down on her sister's head. Gus jumped back and dropped the spoon. Miss Daisy sputtered and pulled the straw from her hair as Miss Violet lunged for her precious wooden spoon.

"Miss Daisy! Are you okay?" Tammy called as she rushed to her side.

"Where is he? I'm going to kill him! Violet Fae, get your recipe for parrot stew. You're mine, bird!" Miss Daisy's eyes zeroed in on where Pierce had Gus in his hands.

"Miss Daisy?" Bridget said kindly, but with a hint of authority as she changed the subject in order to rescue the parrot from the pot. "I don't mean to interrupt, but as you know, Tammy really is in a lot of danger. Mr. and Mrs. Davies were counting on Pierce to help guard her. And so was Ahmed. You wouldn't want to disappoint them, would you?"

"Marcy agreed to this?" Miss Daisy asked hesitantly.

"Yes, in fact she insisted. Tammy is a good friend and I don't want to think about her up there all alone."

"I guess you're right," Miss Daisy finally said. "But you're sleeping on the couch!" With a humph, the sisters walked back into the café and closed the back door.

"Well, now that we got that taken care of, let's get Marko tucked in for the night."

Tammy placed the empty wine glasses in the sink and lounged against the counter as she watched Pierce get ready for bed. He had emerged from the bathroom clean-shaven and smelling of soap. His jeans and t-shirt hung over the end of her couch as he walked across her bedroom in his tight black trunk boxer briefs.

"Are you coming to bed, sweetheart?" he called out to her.

"I thought you were supposed to sleep on the couch," she teased.

"Only if you sleep with me. I promised to guard you and what better way than to have you wrapped in my arms all night?"

"Sounds heavenly. Pierce," Tammy asked slowly, "are you worried at all?"

"I'm only scared about losing you. As long as you're by my side, then all my dreams can come true. Are you afraid, sweetheart?" Pierce placed his hands on the counter on each side of her body.

"Would you think less of me if I said yes?" Tammy asked quietly.

Pierce waited until she raised her head and looked him in the eyes. "Sweetheart, you're the bravest person I know. Come on, let's get you to bed," he said with a wicked grin and a twinkle in his hazel eyes.

In the darkness of the night, the two figures smashed the window and reached inside the door to flip the lock. They quickly ducked into the small kitchen of the apartment over the store, Southern Charms.

"You look here. I'll look in the back. It's a black laptop and a bundle of handwritten notes in a folder. We have to have them to get the details to claim the Cropbot as ours," the man whispered.

The figures spread out and canvassed the apartment. "Do you have anything?" he called from the bedroom.

"There's nothing here!" They had pulled out drawers, looked in cabinets, and under the mattress.

"Dammit. We need to find them and destroy them. It'll cost us tens of millions if we don't," he said as he searched through one of the closets. "I found it!" He pulled out a laptop and turned it on.

"There! Personal Research Notes. Click on that."

"Crap. It's password-protected."

"Well, you're the computer genius. Hack it."

"What do you think I'm trying to do?" he bit back.

"Wait! Do you hear that?"

They strained their ears and heard the door to the shop downstairs open. "Hurry, let's get out of here." He slammed the laptop closed and shoved it into his bag. They ran for the kitchen door and escaped down the stairs as the door to the apartment opened.

CHAPTER FIFTEEN

Pierce lay silent in the darkness of Tammy's apartment and let his mind wander. Marko was snoring softly from his place on the couch and Tammy slept peacefully on Pierce's arm. Slowly, Pierce fell into a state of restless sleep. His mind started to race as it felt as if memories were fighting to come forward.

Suddenly he found himself remembering the night after he and Dr. Oldham had tested the Cropbot. The graduate class had gotten together for beers at the campus dive bar. Aiden was there, along with Mrs. Oldham and a couple of the other spouses of his classmates. Tamara Bell was flirting with him as he poured her another glass of beer from the pitcher.

Aiden grabbed the empty pitcher and headed for the bar. Tamara pressed her breast against his arm and laughed at a joke someone from across the table told as Pierce drank the last sip of beer. Looking around to find Aiden and the missing beer pitcher, Pierce found him with his head leaning close to Mrs. Oldham's in the shadows of the far side of the bar. Dr. Oldham's back was to them as they continued their hushed conversation. Aiden looked up and saw Pierce watching them. He quickly ended the conversation and came back to the table with the full pitcher of beer.

Pierce was about to tease the new teacher's assistant but Tamara jiggled with laughter and his baser instincts shifted his attention away from what he had just seen. With his glass refilled,

Pierce gave a silent salute to his mentor. Dr. Oldham winked and in secret they toasted to their future successes.

Tammy slid away from Pierce's warm embrace the next morning. Pierce looked exhausted and she didn't want to wake him. She crept out of her bedroom and shut the door. She grabbed his shirt from the end of the couch and slid it on over her head. The shirt reached her knees as she padded barefoot into the kitchen to make breakfast for them both.

Gus yawned and stretched his wings and Marko leapt off the couch and followed her into the kitchen in hopes of snagging a morning treat. Tammy turned on her playlist and danced to Blake Shelton as she cooked bacon and eggs. She couldn't stop grinning, knowing she was making it for the naked Pierce in her bed. After all those years of dreaming and wondering, she now knew that it was so much better than she had hoped for.

Unfortunately, not even a night of mind-blowing, earth-shattering, "Oh.My.God!" sex could make her forget that she was a walking target. The wait was brutal. Even though she felt safe with Pierce and knew Ahmed and his minions were outside, she couldn't help but wish the move would be made so it would be all over. No matter how much had been resolved, she still felt that she and Pierce couldn't move forward with their relationship until the men were caught and they were out of danger.

Marko's ears raised and his head popped up a second before a knock sounded on her front door. Tammy knew who it was from the way his tail wagged as he raced to the door. Tammy turned off the stove and put the bacon on a plate before opening the door for Bridget.

"What is that?" Tammy asked of the large box with a big bow stuck on the top.

"This is a gift from Annie and me," Bridget said with a smile. Before she could continue, her mouth formed an *O*. Tammy just hoped Pierce hadn't walked out of the bedroom naked. Bridget pointed behind where Tammy stood. Tammy turned around expecting to see Pierce standing there in his birthday suit only to find herself similarly stunned into silence. "Um, Tammy, is Gus riding on top of Marko or am I just seeing things?" Bridget asked.

Tammy took in the scene of Gus holding on tightly to Marko's collar as the dog trotted into the kitchen and sidled up to the counter. Gus let go of the collar while his tiny feet still grasped at fur and climbed up Marko's neck and onto his head. Gus stretched and the tip of his beak was able to snag the end of a piece of bacon. Pulling it down, he snapped it in half and dropped some to Marko.

"Aw, that's a good bird," Gus laughed as K-9 and bird enjoyed the stolen treat.

"That didn't just happen, did it?" Bridget asked.

"I don't even know what to say," Tammy replied.

"The guys at the training facility would never believe me. Come on, Marko, we're meeting Annie at the high school to sweep for drugs. Should be fun!" Bridget handed the big rectangular box to Tammy and headed out the door with Marko by her side.

"Awww," Gus squawked sadly as he climbed back up his cage to his perch. Tammy shook her head and tore off the bow to her present. Whatever it was, it was heavy.

"Morning, babe," Pierce said as he sauntered out of the bedroom. "You look good in that shirt." He grinned as he zipped his jeans and headed over to give her a kiss. "What's on the agenda today? Breakfast in bed?" he asked as he wrapped his arms around her waist and pulled her in for a kiss meant to sway her to his idea.

"Nope." Tammy said, setting down the box and heading into the kitchen. "Breakfast and then a day at the office—a day at the office in which you stay out of sight. I need to stay visible and accessible. Also, I got a text from Ahmed. He's meeting us at the office. He said he has some more information he thought you'd want to know about before he has Marshall turn it over to the detectives."

"I wonder what it is? All I know is that this can't be over soon enough."

"Do you think this all has to do with your invention? Which, by the way, is very impressive. I had no idea you were so talented," Tammy told him as she set the plates of eggs and bacon on the small kitchen table.

"I'm talented at many things," Pierce winked. "But, seriously, thank you. That means a lot. It was a lot of hard work and very late nights. So far the testing has been better than I could've ever hoped for. If Dr. Oldham hadn't been killed, then I would've debuted the Cropbot this fall and, hopefully, gotten the financial backing necessary to start mass production of them for spring planting season." Pierce paused as he thought about his future. "If this gets wrapped up and my patent is cleared, I still want to do that. But, to answer your question, yes. I think this is all about my invention. It has to be."

Pierce finished his breakfast and took a shower while Tammy got ready. He'd never really spent a lot of time with a woman before in a domestic situation and he had to admit, it was really nice. He liked that they worked well together. She cooked and he cleaned. She got dressed while he showered. It all seemed so easy, so comfortable. There was something secure in it.

It ended too soon, he thought, as they walked into Henry's office. Kenna popped her head out and called hello before she hurried off to court with Dani. Tammy looked very professional today in a black pantsuit. It made him feel a little underdressed in his jeans.

"Hey. Glad you're both still alive," Henry said with a grin as he strode out of his office and into the lobby.

"You think I'd fail at my job?"

Henry jumped. "Where the hell did you come from?" He asked Ahmed who was casually standing in the doorway that led back to the offices.

Ahmed just looked at him and then turned to Tammy. "Good morning, my dear." He kissed her cheek and then headed over to shake Pierce's hand.

"So, what did you find?" Pierce asked anxiously.

"Someone broke into your temporary housing last night," Ahmed told him.

"What?"

"They searched the apartment, rather amateurishly, I might add, after breaking a window to get in. That set off an alarm and Cole responded with one of my men. It appears that nothing was taken."

"Do you know who did it?" Tammy asked.

"I have a very good idea. You know the ghosting program I told you about that I found on Dr. Oldham's computer?" When everyone nodded, Ahmed continued. "Well, I put a very similar program on Pierce's computer at home. Last night someone tried to break the code for the Personal Research Notes file."

"I don't have a file labeled that," Pierce told them.

"You do now," Ahmed said smoothly.

"So, what good did that do?" Henry asked impatiently.

"When an incorrect password is entered, it activates the camera on your laptop and starts to record. I have video of the couple who broke into your apartment," Ahmed told them with a hint of smugness as he pulled out his tablet and pressed Play.

Pierce watched as a man's face came into focus. It was covered by a black ski mask. A second, smaller person came into view over the first's shoulder. Pierce listened to the voices. There was something so familiar, but his mind was racing too fast for him to place it.

"Could they be who you saw the other night leaving Pierce's house?" Henry asked Tammy as he watched the video and listened to the two criminals bicker.

"It could be. But I'm just not sure," Tammy responded.

"There's more," Ahmed said. "I traced the ghosting program on Dr. Oldham's computer to a computer in the school's research lab."

Pierce turned his eyes to Ahmed's face. The pieces were falling into place. Now he just needed confirmation. "Whose?"

"Aiden Fink."

"That's him. I knew that voice." Pierce tapped the screen on the tablet at the frozen figure of the larger man trying to hack the computer. "And that," he said pointing to the smaller figure, "is no man. That is Mrs. Oldham. Son of a bitch!" Pierce yelled as he slammed his hand on the desk. "They set me up and killed Dr. Oldham so they could get my patent!"

"That's what I thought, too," Ahmed confirmed.

"How could I be so stupid? It's all right here," Pierce tapped his head, "but I still can't get it out. I now even know who it was and I still can't freaking remember!" Pierce started pacing. His heart was racing, his head hurt, and he was mad.

"Don't worry, you'll remember," Tammy said kindly as she placed her hand on his arm.

Pierce jerked away in anger. "No! I'm not. That's the thing. I'm not remembering anything! I need a break. Ahmed, watch Tammy. I'm going for a drive before I do or say something I'll regret." Pierce slammed the front door before Tammy could follow.

"Pierce!" Tammy called as she hurried after him.

"Tammy, don't," Ahmed said quietly as he gently grabbed her arm and stopped her from chasing after Pierce. "A man needs some time alone to work things out sometimes."

"This is great, Ahmed. I don't know how you did it," Henry praised as he walked out of the conference room completely unfazed by Pierce's outburst.

"And you don't know where it came from either," Ahmed said sternly as Henry nodded in acknowledgment. This evidence was going to be anonymously left by the door of the office as far as the police were concerned.

"I'll call the police now to tell them what I found by the door when I got to work this morning."

"No, wait. Let Pierce calm down and talk to him about it first. This can be left at any time."

"Sure, just tell me when." Henry shook Ahmed's hand and then disappeared back into his office.

"Are you alright, dear?" Ahmed asked gently.

"No! I'm upset. I'm sad, hurt, and pissed all at once," Tammy said through gritted teeth. She turned and headed back to her desk when the bell over the door rang. Hoping Pierce had stopped being such a man, she turned and felt the emotions bubble over.

"I thought I'd bring Prissy Pig down to guard you at the office," Old Man Tabby said as he walked into the lobby with the largest pink pig she'd ever seen wearing a pink rhinestone collar and leash. Tears spilled over and Ahmed wrapped his arms around her.

"Thank you for your concern, Mr. Tabernacle. That is very thoughtful of you. Why don't you put," Ahmed paused and gathered himself, "Prissy against the back door."

"Will do. She's a good girl, she is." Old Man Tabby trotted the pig into the back. Tammy even managed a laugh as she heard Henry gasp at the site of a pig walking past his office.

"Let me take you to lunch to get your mind off Pierce for a while," Ahmed suggested.

"Thanks, but I think I'd rather just crash at my apartment. I ate a late breakfast and I don't think I can handle a lot of company right now."

Ahmed nodded and silently handed Tammy her purse before opening the door for her. Tammy smiled grimly and headed out of the office with Ahmed by her side.

CHAPTER SIXTEEN

Tammy was quiet as she and Ahmed walked down Main Street. She finally voiced her concerns as she approached the café. "What do you think of everything going on? Do I need to be worried?"

"We need to be vigilant. They didn't find what they were looking for. I expect their actions to escalate until they have what they want, you dead and Pierce's patent. The only question is whether they'll go after you both."

Ahmed slowed as he approached the open back door to the café. He held up his hand to silently instruct Tammy to stop. Slowly he crept forward and looked around the doorframe into Miss Violet's kitchen.

Ahmed raised his finger to his lips and gestured for Tammy to hurry. Tammy quickly shot past the open door and started up the stairs to her apartment. "You are so busted!"

"How so?" Ahmed asked, confused.

"You're worried about being hit by a frying pan!" Tammy teased.

Ahmed simply raised an eyebrow and held out his hand for her keys.

"Scaredy-cat," she taunted.

"I'd hate to embarrass them. Wait." Ahmed's whole body changed. Normally he was relaxed with a hint of lethal, like a gun with the safety on. But now the safety was off. His whole body radiated deadly intent.

"What is it?" Tammy choked out in fear. Nothing seemed off, but the change in Ahmed's voice and body language was enough to have her seriously freaked out.

"Someone broke into your apartment. There's a tiny scratch mark on the lock that wasn't there before. Now, be quiet and stand behind me. I think we're about to find out about those threats you were worried about." Ahmed put his hand on the knob and slowly turned it.

Pierce turned up the music and tried to calm down. The feeling of betrayal washed over him as he pressed harder on the gas pedal. He had considered Aiden a friend, and all this time he was trying to steal Pierce's invention. Not only that, but he murdered their mentor and friend. How was Mrs. Oldham involved? It still didn't make sense to him. The blackness clouded his memories as he tried to force them forward. If only he could remember. If only he could know for sure it was Aiden who had tied him up and tried to kill him with the house fire. If only…

He zoomed past the countryside on the narrow two-lane road and tried to breathe in the fresh air. The smell of wildflowers and fresh-cut grass drifted in his window as he drove out toward his parents' farm. A couple of rounds on the bull would help him achieve some clarity. Then he'd call Henry and Ahmed to discuss what to do next. Hell, the detectives were probably already aware of the information. By the time Pierce relaxed, they may already be in custody.

The birds chirped and cows mooed in the distant pastures hugging the road. As much as he tried to channel his anger, it still didn't work. Realizing he was going way too fast to take the curve in the road, he pressed on the brake to slow down.

"Shit!" Pierce pumped the brake and nothing happened. He pressed it to the floor as he headed straight for the sharp curve. The brakes didn't work and he was approaching too fast.

Cranking the wheel, he tried to take the turn. His front passenger side tire hit the gravel on the side of the road and he lost control of the truck. It shot forward across the road and headed straight for the wood fence holding a herd of cows. Dirt and grass shot into the air as the tires tore through it. Pierce felt his heart stop as the front of the truck broke through the four-board fence. The top plank shattered in two, sending the board through the windshield straight at Pierce's head.

Tammy held her breath as she watched Ahmed pull out a gun from the small of his back. He slowly pushed the door open and silently slid into her apartment. Tammy's legs trembled as she took a step forward. She stopped on the threshold and looked around her tiny living space. Nothing seemed to be out of place. It looked exactly as it had that morning, except now everything seemed sinister. Was her apartment always cast in shadows? Had that flower vase been moved? Her pink curtains looked as if they were ghosts haunting her living room now.

Tammy shook her head. She was being ridiculous. She closed her eyes and opened them again. Ahmed stood inside the door listening to the sounds of the apartment as she looked again with new eyes. Everything was fine. The pretty curtains were tied back with pink bows, the couch was beautiful in its new slipcover, and the flowers she put in the vase yesterday had filled the apartment with a lovely aroma. She was just about to relax and walk all the way inside when she noticed Gus was agitated.

Gus was pacing around on the top of his cage. "Aw, bad bird! Bad bird!" was all the warning she got before gunfire erupted. Tammy hit the ground hard as Ahmed ducked behind the entertainment center and returned the gunfire coming from her bedroom. Tammy felt her heart pounding. Her eyes were wild as she watched Ahmed calmly reload. He wasn't even breathing heavily.

"My dear, it may be a good idea to head down to the café," Ahmed said to her calmly. Tammy looked at him as if he were from another planet. What did he say? She couldn't hear him over the thundering in her ears. She saw his lips moving, so he must've said something. Ahmed repeated the order and finally it penetrated her thought.

"Oh! Downstairs, right!" Without thinking Tammy stood up, but before she could get out the door a second figure in black jumped up from behind her kitchen counter and fired right at her chest.

Ahmed turned at the sound of a second shooter. He saw the shot connect with Tammy's chest as the force of the bullet knocked her to the ground where she lay motionless. An unfamiliar rage took over. He'd been through many things and seen such horrors that nightmares couldn't even touch. However, he had always been able to stay disconnected, calm, and in control. That's what made him so good at his job.

But not now. Now rage consumed him. He narrowed his eyes and charged the man that dared hurt the closest thing to a little sister he had. He ran straight at him, emptying his clip. The shots hit the man in the gut and the leg as he gave up trying to fire back and leapt through the kitchen window. Glass shattered and rained down on the street. The man howled in pain as a leg snapped when he hit the sidewalk.

"Tammy!" He heard Miss Violet's elderly voice scream in panic. He thought about leaping out the window after the man, but when he saw the first man in black slide their car to a stop and toss his partner inside, he knew now he needed to do everything he could to save Tammy.

He turned around to see that half the town had managed to fill the tiny apartment. They carried guns, forks, and an apple cobbler. Emotions flooded him as he saw Miss Daisy press her fingers to Tammy's neck to check for a pulse. He blindly pushed people out of the way as he hurried to Tammy's side. She just had to be alive, he told himself as dread filled him.

Annie Davies hung up the phone at the sheriff's station and pushed back her chair. She had serious police business to discuss with Marshall. Annie walked back into his office and plopped down in the chair across from where Marshall sat at his desk.

"We have a serious crime spree going on," Annie said dryly.

"What is it this time? Does Edna think someone is going through her garbage again?"

"Nope, a rash of out-of-control teenagers are tipping cows. Got two calls about it this morning." Annie smiled. Life was a lot different as a sheriff's deputy in a small town compared to her days as an undercover DEA agent. But, she wouldn't change it for the world.

"I hate having to go after kids for stuff I did when I was that age. It seems so..." Marshall paused and Annie sat up in her seat. "Was that gunfire?"

"Yes, it was," Annie replied as she leapt up from the chair and unlocked the sheriff department's arsenal. She grabbled a Remington 700P light tactical rifle and tossed it to Marshall as he strode past her. Annie grabbed herself one and they ran out the door in time to see a man come crashing through the window above the café.

"Freeze or I will shoot you!" Annie yelled as she raised the gun to take aim. A car came sliding to a stop and the driver got out and shoved the man inside. "It's been a while since I shot someone, I'm kinda itchy to do so again!" The driver paused and looked at her from across the hood of the car.

"Put your hands up, asshole!" Marshall's voice boomed as he and Annie crept forward with the rifles raised. The man looked between them and then leapt into the car. The tires smoked as he gunned it. Marshall and Annie opened fire. Bullets bit into the trunk of the car as it sped away.

"Dammit! I got a plate, though. What the hell was that all about?" Marshall asked as he looked up to the broken window.

"I don't know, but it can't be good. The café's empty." They looked at each other and Annie felt her face drain of blood. "Oh God, Tammy!"

Annie and Marshall started running across the street when Dinky's cruiser slid to a stop in front of them with the sirens wailing. "Sheriff! A 9-1-1 call just came in."

"I know, we shot at them, but didn't get them. We're going to see how Tammy is now," Marshall said as he hurried around the cruiser on his way to the back of the café.

"No, sir, it's your brother. Something's happened to Pierce."

CHAPTER SEVENTEEN

Betsy Ashton had the top down on her convertible as the wind whipped at the silk horseshoe scarf she had tied over her head. She was heading back to the farm after spending the morning at Keeneland Race Track watching her horses train. They had a nice boy who had finished fourth at the Derby and third in the Preakness. He was now preparing for the Belmont. While they didn't think he'd do as well as Naked Boot Leg did a couple of years back, she did think he'd be in the front half of the field.

She slowed her car as she rounded a particularly sharp curve on the small country road and slammed on her brakes. A truck lay smoking in the middle of the fence line. A board from the fence was protruding from the driver's side windshield and she couldn't see if the driver was still inside.

Betsy pulled her car to a stop and hurried over to the truck. She looked in the passenger window and gasped. The fence board was lodged into the driver's headrest. The airbag had deployed, but now it hung limp with blood splattered across it. Recognition hit her as she tried to pry open the door.

"Pierce! Honey, answer me!"

Pierce heard the sweetest voice anxiously calling his name. His eyes fluttered open and his head felt as if it had been split in two.

He groaned as his eyes adjusted to the light. His sunglasses were smashed and soft hands were patting his face.

"Oh thank goodness! Pierce, honey, you've been in a car accident. You're bleeding heavily and you might have hurt your head when the airbag deployed. I've called 9-1-1, but I need to try to stop the bleeding. Can you hold still for a moment while I wrap this around your neck?" Betsy pulled off her scarf and Pierce finally felt the blood that Betsy had mentioned running down his neck.

"My brakes. They didn't work." His mind raced. Someone had cut them. It had to be intentional. He kept his trucks in excellent condition. There was no way they just failed on their own. "Ow!" he cried out as Betsy tightened the scarf around his neck.

"I'm sorry, honey," she cooed softly. Her voice was so calm he figured it couldn't be that bad. He turned his head and saw the board from the fence impaled on the bottom on the headrest. It appeared to have come through the window, nicking the side of the airbag and deflating it as it sliced through the side of his neck before being stopped by the headrest. If the board had been just a little more to the left, it could've decapitated him. He was lucky it hadn't hit his artery or he'd have bled out in seconds.

"Thank you, Betsy. I wonder if I can get out?" Pierce tried his door, but it was pinned shut by a heavy fence post.

"I think you'd have to get out this way, but it's best that you wait until the EMTs get here and help you out." Betsy turned her head and waved. "Reinforcements have arrived. Just stay calm and we'll get you out in a jiffy."

Marshall slammed on the brakes and left his car, lights flashing, in the middle of the jam-packed road. Ambulances, fire trucks, his parents' truck, Betsy's convertible, and John Wolfe's car all sat blocking the road.

"Pierce!" Marshall ran toward his little brother who was sitting on the back of the ambulance flanked by Marcy and Betsy. Betsy's white pants were covered with blood along with her peach blouse. His father, Cade, and John stood off just a little bit, looking at Pierce's truck with serious expressions.

"I'm okay. But, it was them. I know it was. I went to press on the brakes and nothing. They were gone. I lost control and went through the fence."

"There's a hole in the brake line allowing the fluid to leak out so that he'd probably be out of town before the brakes failed," Jake said as the guys came to stand with them.

"How are you? Are you hurt badly?" Marshall asked, eyeing the bandage around his neck and his blackening eyes.

"The airbag caused the black eyes. Seatbelt bruised along my chest. And the fence board tried to take my head off, but only managed a little cut." Pierce tried to pawn it off as nothing, but it had scared the hell out of him.

Marshall looked at Betsy. "That doesn't look like a little cut."

"Okay, so it isn't so little. But it also wasn't as bad as it could've been." Pierce knew he could've easily died and he was done talking about it. He was alive and he'd never felt so thankful. All he wanted to do was curl up in the impossibly tiny bed of Tammy's and have her play nurse. "Where's Tammy? Did you tell her I was all right? I don't want her to worry."

Pierce saw the change come over Marshall immediately. "What is it, Marshall?" Pierce said in a tone that brokered no debate.

"Pierce, Tammy's been shot." Pierce didn't know how to process what Marshall just told him. Shot? Marcy and Betsy gasped and John looked down at his feet and kicked the dirt. That old goat knew and didn't tell him!

"Is she…" Pierce couldn't say the word. She couldn't be dead, just couldn't be.

"I don't know," Marshall said quietly. "I was in such a hurry to get to you I haven't checked in with Annie. I don't even know exactly what happened."

Pierce felt his blood pressure spike. Adrenaline poured into his system as he leapt up and punched Marshall in the face, sending him sprawling onto the ground. "The woman I'm madly in love with is shot and you don't think to check to see if she's even alive!" Pierce yelled down at his brother.

"I'm sorry, I was slightly more concerned to find out if my own brother was alive!" Marshall shot up from the ground and pushed Pierce back a few steps.

"I don't care about me! Just get me to her now!" Pierce shoved past him and got into the cruiser as Marshall hurried after him. Marshall sped away as Marcy and Betsy shared a knowing look. Pierce had fallen hard.

Ahmed knelt down beside Tammy as Annie rushed into the room. People moved out of the way as she pushed her way forward. Miss Violet was wiping away the tears in her eyes as she knelt down next to Ahmed. "Is she..."

"Tammy!" Henry shouted as he burst into the room. The crowd had moved back as those closest to Tammy had tried to help her.

Ahmed looked her over in puzzlement. Three bullet holes with gunpowder residue were clear as day on her chest, but there wasn't any blood. Hesitantly, he felt the entry points of her wounds. His breath rushed out of him and he felt dizzy as he looked up to see Henry eyeing him curiously. Henry reached down and felt the bullet holes. He grabbed the top of her blouse and tore it open.

"I see she got our present," Annie said with relief.

"That's the ugliest, and at the same time the most beautiful undergarment I've ever seen!" Henry laughed as he loosened the Velcro on the bulletproof vest.

Tammy fought the panic caused by the darkness swallowing her. From the depths of her mind, a voice was dragging her back. She listened to his calm, silky voice guiding her out of the darkness.

"Tammy, my dear. You're safe. You can wake up now." Ahmed stroked her head gently as Tammy woke.

"Did you get them?" she mumbled as she looked around at all the faces filled with relief above her. Some still had napkins stuffed in their shirts and sandwiches in their hands from the café. The Rose sisters squeezed her hands as their eyes shined with happy tears.

"No. They escaped. But I shot one…twice. He won't live long." Ahmed said with no emotion.

"You're slipping," Tammy teased as she tried to sit up. She looked down at her blouse, which was torn and pushed open, exposing the three bullets lodged in her vest above her heart. "This was my favorite blouse. Who tore it?"

"I'm sorry, I did that," Henry grimaced.

"Well, you always said my shirt would look good on the bedroom floor. Too bad I wasn't shot ten feet that way and your pick-up line would have finally worked!"

Tammy tried to laugh as she nodded toward her bedroom, but it hurt way too much. Her joke worked, though, as Henry roared with laughter and the crowd joined in. The laughter was therapeutic as the relief from the tense situation settled the room.

"Tammy!" A voice yelled over the laughter.

"Pierce! I'm here!" The crowd parted and Pierce rushed in with Marshall right behind him. "Oh my God! What happened to you?" The crowd gasped as they took in the blood seeping through the bandage around his neck and his two black eyes. The tension that had just been dispersed by laughter returned and hung heavy among the group.

Tammy tried to stand up but winced in pain. "We need to get you to the hospital immediately."

"Ambulance is waiting downstairs," Bridget told them as she walked into the overcrowded apartment. She looked down at Tammy with a blank face. "I'm glad you wore our present."

"You got her the vest?" Pierce asked with a hint of surprise.

"Annie and I did. Better than silk panties, huh?"

Tammy snickered at the inside joke and then at the way all the single men and some of the married looked over at Bridget, trying to figure out what she was wearing under the tight brown shirt and camouflaged cargo pants.

Pierce knelt down beside Tammy and placed a soft kiss on her lips. "You scared me, sweetheart. I love you so much. But, now I'm sorry, I need to leave you for a bit."

"What?" Tammy was confused. Leave her, now? Why?

"Noodle, will you and my mom take Tammy to the hospital. Don't leave her side." Noodle nodded and Marcy moved further into the room to help her stand up.

"Come on, dear. Let's get you checked out." Marcy pushed Tammy's hair gently out of her face and put her arm around her as Tammy stood up.

"Where are you going? Pierce, if anyone needs to go to the hospital, it's you."

"You know how men are, dear. They hate doctors. I'm sure Pierce will be there soon. The men have something they need to do." Marcy and Noodle looked at each other over Tammy's head and hurried her out of the apartment before she could figure out what was going on.

Pierce kissed Tammy quickly on the cheek as his mother and Noodle helped her out of the apartment. "I'll be there before you know it. Just feel better for me, love."

The apartment emptied quickly as they sensed what was coming. Soon all that were left were Pierce, Ahmed, Marshall, Henry, and Bridget. Pierce put his hands on his hips and let out a deep breath.

Pierce looked right at Ahmed. "We're ending this now."

CHAPTER EIGHTEEN

Pierce kept his eyes trained on Ahmed as he looked Pierce over. Ahmed nodded ever so slightly.

"I'm coming, too," Marshall said as he unhooked his badge from his jeans and started to unbutton the brown sheriff's shirt he wore while working, exposing a white t-shirt underneath.

"Me, too," Henry said, surprisingly forcefully.

Pierce shook his head. "Sorry, Marshall, you can't. You're too recognizable. And Henry, you can't witness what I'm thinking of doing. No offense, but you're not cut out for this kind of thing."

"I'm not asking, Pierce. I'll come on my own if I have to. But Tammy is the only woman to ever tolerate me and she's the best friend I've got." Henry stood tall, confident, and unwavering.

"Fine." Pierce clipped. He turned to Ahmed and asked, "I've never done anything like this. How do we proceed?"

"Gentlemen," Bridget interrupted calmly. "I'd like to assist in this matter."

Ahmed raised an eyebrow and Marshall's lips quirked. Henry flat out laughed and Bridget simply smiled.

"You want to help us?" Ahmed said with disbelief ringing in his voice.

"Yes. And, I bet each of you I can get a confession in under a minute all while never laying a hand on them," Bridget said definitively.

"Sure, hon. I'll take that bet," Henry snickered.

"I'll bet you, Pierce, for twenty acres of the back part of your property that I can do it." Bridget turned to the rest of the men and continued. "I bet you, Marshall, for the job of exclusive K-9 handler for the sheriff's department. And you, Henry, for the legal work on acquiring the property and setting up a company to train police dogs." Bridget turned then to Ahmed. "From you, I want hand-to-hand combat training and your reference for foreign government jobs."

"And what do we get if you can't follow through with your bet?" Ahmed asked in a slightly disinterested tone.

"Henry, your pick, I'm just not getting naked. Marshall, I'll work Marko for free for the rest of the year. Pierce, I'll recommend your Cropbot to one of the largest manufacturers in the country; I guarded the CEO's family recently. Ahmed, I'll provide protection and explosive sweeps for free for the royal family's next two trips to Kentucky."

The men all looked at each other and then slowly shrugged. "Deal," they all said at once.

"Now, let's go see what you're made of, Miss Springer," Ahmed said before heading out the door.

Pierce walked down the empty hallway of the agriculture building. They had tried both Aiden and Mrs. Oldham's homes. Both were empty. The hall filled with the echo of his party's footsteps as they headed toward his old research lab.

As they neared the room, Pierce heard Aiden toss something against the wall and curse. Pierce slowed as he approached the slightly open door. He looked in through the narrow window and tightened his fists in anger. There sat a copy of his Cropbot. Aiden was kneeling on the floor next to it trying to work on its internal components.

Pierce bit his lip and was about to burst into the room when he felt Ahmed pull him back. With a quiet shake of his head, Ahmed warned Pierce to stay quiet. Ahmed pushed his way into the lab with Pierce in tow. Marshall and Henry stayed at the door waiting to give Bridget her signal to enter. Aiden looked up with irritation until he saw Pierce. Then his eyes went wide before he could mask them.

Aiden quickly stood, palming a screwdriver as he stepped in front of the Cropbot in a failed attempt to hide it from view. "What are you doing here?" Aiden shot accusingly at Pierce as his eyes darted from person to person.

Pierce waited until Henry pulled out his cell phone subtly and hit Record. "Interesting piece of equipment there. That looks amazingly like my invention to which I hold a patent." Pierce paused, trying to keep his voice even before he started again, "and it matches the personal notes I have on my laptop that was nearly hacked last night during a break-in."

Aiden's face turned red with anger. He stepped forward menacingly, "You think it was me? You're accusing me of theft?" Aiden shouted.

"I don't need to accuse you of it. The evidence is right there behind you. Do you actually dare to deny it?" Pierce laughed to the others at the absurdity of Aiden's dismissal.

"You arrogant son of a bitch!" Aiden again stepped forward angrily, holding the screwdriver as if it were a knife.

Bridget took her cue and stepped forward with Marko. "Sir, this is a trained police dog. Lower your weapon or I'll set him on you."

Aiden turned toward her without lowering the screwdriver, the anger clear on his face. Bridget dropped Marko's leash and gave the command. Marko sprang forward, charging across the room with his teeth bared as he barked and growled. Bridget gave another command and Marko stopped in front of Aiden who stood rooted to the ground. Marko was less than a foot away barking and snarling at Aiden. Sweat broke out along his face as he watched Marko.

"You need to drop the weapon, sir, or I'll have him remove it from your grasp," Bridget said calmly. Aiden dropped the weapon and Bridget gave Marko another command. "You know, I saw something just like this—only working, just a week ago. Are you sure you didn't steal this?"

"I'm sure," Aiden stuttered. Marko growled softly and a drop of sweat rolled down the side of Aiden's face.

"Well, there you have it, gentlemen. It wasn't him," Bridget said happily.

Ahmed shot her a look of confusion and Pierce flat out looked at her as if she were growing horns.

"Of course it's him!" Pierce flung a copy of the picture of Aiden in a mask at him. Aiden's reaction gave him away as he looked at the picture on the cold tile floor.

"That's not me!" Aiden cried.

"Well, you see the confusion then, sir. But I have a simple way of solving this." Bridget reached into her bag and pulled out Pierce's laptop. "Marko, *hier plaats.*" Marko immediately ran to Bridget and sat down in front of her. She then lowered the laptop to his level.

"What are you doing?" Aiden asked nervously as Marko started sniffing the laptop.

"He's smelling the laptop and will then track the scent he receives off of it. The man in the picture left his scent on this computer. If it isn't you, then you don't have anything to worry about," Bridget said with a polite smile on her face.

"Marko, *keuring!*" Marko sniffed in the air, turned around, and ran straight for Aiden. He immediately sat in front of Aiden, never moving, not even blinking as he stared him down.

"Well, Mr. Fink, isn't it? That's a positive indication of scent. You have definitely touched this computer recently." Bridget pulled out a tennis ball from her pocket and tossed it for Marko who happily chased it down and brought it back to her. "Sheriff Davies, I do believe that's probable cause for an arrest. You may want to call in local reinforcement. They are quite eager to hang someone out to dry for Dr. Oldham's murder. They'll be thrilled with the evidence against Aiden here."

"Wait! Murder? I didn't murder anyone!" Aiden cried.

"Oh, I'm pretty sure you did. See, we have a waiter who can identify you driving Pierce home the night of the murder. Plus Tammy can identify you fleeing Pierce's house. Then trying to murder her today, too, doesn't look too good. You'll be lucky if you don't get the needle." Bridget hardened her voice and Marko leaped up and started to growl again at her aggressive tone.

Aiden flinched and then paled. "I swear I don't know what you're talking about."

Marko growled again and Bridget just shrugged. "Sorry, after Marko identified your smell, I don't believe a word you say."

Aiden looked wide-eyed from Marko to Pierce to Bridget. "Okay! Okay! We did steal Pierce's invention and we broke into his house trying to find his personal notes. I can't get the electronics to work!"

"Who's we? You know if your accomplice committed the murder, then you're still culpable," Bridget warned. Marko barked loudly this time and Aiden jumped back. "I wouldn't do that. Sudden movements aren't very wise."

"It was Suzy Oldham. It was all her idea. She flipped out when she discovered her husband was hiding the fact that he helped you with the invention and didn't get his name on it. But she didn't *kill* him! She came to me and suggested we steal it! I swear!"

"That's strange, I wonder why she'd come to you?" Bridget asked.

"We were having an affair. It started three years ago. She got me the position here with her husband so we could see each other more. It was all her idea! We even talked about it the night Dr. Oldham was murdered – that's why I know she didn't do it. She was with me. Please, believe me," Aiden begged.

Bridget hooked the leash back on Marko. She looked over to Henry who silently turned off the camera and then to Ahmed who looked down at his watch.

"Fifty-four seconds."

"Well, welcome to Keeneston, Miss Springer. It'll be a pleasure having you and Marko on the team," Marshall said as he pulled out his cell phone and called the detectives.

"What's going on? You believe me, don't you?" Aiden cried in bewilderment.

"Yeah, I actually do. You're still going to jail, though," Pierce shrugged. "Now, the real question is who murdered Dr. Oldham and why?"

Tammy flinched as Dr. Emma Francis pressed the dark marks on her chest. With Emma's help, Tammy was able to convince Marcy and Noodle to stay outside the exam room as she stripped out of her shirt and bra. The whole area above her heart was various colors of black, blue, and green.

"You're lucky it wasn't a direct hit to your heart or you could've bruised it. We won't know for sure until we do an MRI, but I think you're just going to be very sore for a while. It doesn't feel as if anything was broken." Emma shook her head and her dark brown curls bounced. "Thank goodness you had that vest on!"

"I know. Bridget and Annie gave it to me, I think mostly as a joke, but I decided as I was walking out the door to see what was in the package Bridget had dropped off. I couldn't resist trying it on. The only reason I kept it on was I noticed how late I was for work," Tammy explained as she pulled on a hospital gown.

"I bet Pierce is so relieved. Noodle told me that you all made it official by having dinner at the café the other night," Emma smiled and Tammy was grateful to be speaking of something other than the shooting.

"I'm sure he is. He ran off to do something, though, and that has me very worried. I just wish he'd have come with me."

"I'll stop by tonight to check on you both if you'd like. I'm spending most of my nights in Keeneston now anyway," Emma blushed and Tammy laughed.

"So you and Noodle are getting serious?" Tammy teased.

Emma pulled off her exam gloves and held out her hand. There was a beautiful diamond on her ring finger. "He gave me it this morning. He had it hooked on his fishing line. I saw it sparkling on the ground when I woke up. I went to reach for it and he reeled in the line with me following behind!" Tears glistened in Emma's eyes as she smiled. "Then he got down on one knee and said that he knew a good catch when he saw it. He just wished I wouldn't throw him back in. Then he told me how much he loved me and how I was his everything. Finally, as tears streamed down my face, he asked me to marry him."

Tammy moved as quickly as her bruised body would let her and wrapped her arms around Emma. "Congratulations! I feel so honored you told me! You two are so perfect for each other."

Emma wiped a tear from her eye. "Well, now that I have you smiling, let's get that MRI done and get you home to spread the gossip!"

Tammy walked out of the emergency room and into the lobby of the hospital with Marcy and Noodle by her side. Marcy had her arm wrapped protectively around her as they stopped in front of the small crowd gathered in the lobby.

Mo, Annie, and Nabi stood up and came over to greet her. Nabi moved to the door and gave a signal out the window. Mo and Annie hurried over, firing off questions on how she was feeling. Tammy smiled and tried not to be overwhelmed.

"I'm okay, just very sore. I need a day or two of lying in bed and then I'll be back to normal." Tammy reached for Annie's hand and squeezed it. "I wouldn't be alive without that gift. How can I thank you?"

"By resting and feeling better." Annie gave her a grim smile and Tammy realized this wasn't over by a long shot.

"We're ready, Your Highness," Nabi said in all seriousness as he bowed quickly to Mo.

"Nabi! How sweet of you to come check on me. I didn't know you cared so much!" Tammy teased.

"It's Nabi Ulmalhamsh Mosteghanemi," Mini-Ahmed clipped out.

Mo just shook his head and Annie rolled her eyes as Tammy burst out giggling.

"Come, my dear. I have the limo waiting to take you home." Mo said as Nabi opened the glass door for him to escort Tammy out.

"Please, get in first. I'm just moving a little slow." Tammy looked up to mini-Ahmed and smiled. "I'm sure your man here will help a damsel in distress get slowly to the limo." Tammy looked across the emergency drive to where the limo was parked and kicked herself for being so stubborn as to turn down the wheelchair.

Mo nodded and took Marcy's arm and led her to the limo. Noodle and Annie would follow them in the cruiser as they hurried off to get the car.

"Alone at last," Tammy teased Nabi. He just looked at her and the only indication that he had heard her was the slight stumble in his step. Tammy smiled. Mission complete!

Tammy held onto Nabi's arm tightly as they started across the ambulance bay when the roar of an engine caused Tammy to look up. Fear gripped her, but before she could move Nabi grabbed her around the waist and lifted her off the ground. Without saying a word, he tucked her head into his shoulder and dove for the sliding emergency room doors as the ambulance barreled toward them.

Tammy heard Marcy shriek the second before they hit the ground. Nabi cradled Tammy's head as he turned in the air, taking the force of the hit before rolling on top of her to protect her. Nurses and doctors flooded into the lobby as the ambulance bounced off the sidewalk and sideswiped another car before tearing off down the street.

"Why, Nabi!" Tammy gasped as she tried to fill her lungs with oxygen. "You do like me!" While Nabi remained expressionless, he didn't correct her on his name. Tammy felt triumphant until the realization that this wasn't an accident came crashing down on her.

"Oh Nabi, I'm so sorry, but I think I'm about to cry." Tammy felt the tears fill her eyes and she finally let go with a body-wrenching sob. She was really starting to dislike trying to be killed.

"Oh, no! Don't. Please. Will you stop if I let you call me Nabi from now on?"

Tammy giggled and her tears started to slow as Mo and Marcy helped her up.

"Oh, Mrs. Davies! We need to find Pierce. If they're doing all this to me, we have to warn Pierce that he's in danger." Suddenly the fact that she was nearly run over didn't seem to matter. Tammy had to get to Pierce. She had to know that he was all right.

"Well done, Nabi Ulmalhamsh Mosteghanemi. You proved yourself very worthy of your duty today," Mo said as he shook Nabi's hand. "Tammy, you are coming home to stay with us."

Tammy shook her head. "Thank you, Mo, but I don't want to put you and Dani in danger, especially with her pregnant. I couldn't stand it if anything happened because of me. Besides, I'm sure the Rose sisters and the rest of the café will be on high alert now. If I'm going to be on the defensive, I'd rather do it from my apartment."

Mo looked at her and grabbed her hand in his. "Are you sure I can't convince you to stay at my house?"

"I'm sure. Thank you. You're such a dear friend," Tammy kissed his cheek and Mo patted her hand.

"Let's get you home, my dear."

CHAPTER NINETEEN

Tammy looked out the tinted window of the limousine and cringed. She was tired and hungry, but the café was packed. All the tables were taken and people were just floating from table to table talking. Talking about her. Oh, she now felt so bad for all the times she did it!

"I can take you around back?" Mo said, but the normal confidence in his voice was now filled with skepticism.

"It's alright. I better go face the crowd head on. At least Miss Violet will feed me." Tammy turned to where Marcy sat across from her on the cool, soft leather seat. "Have you heard anything yet?" Marcy had a death grip on a cell phone in her lap.

"Not yet, dear. But I'll let you know as soon as I do." Marcy leaned over and gave Tammy's leg a pat. "Such a good girl you are. Your father never knew how lucky he had it," Marcy said before the door opened and Nabi helped her out.

Tammy took a fortifying breath and climbed out of the climate-controlled limousine and into the warm spring air. Summer was coming soon. But for the next few weeks, Keeneston was enjoying perfect weather. Trees were in bloom, flowers overflowed from pots, and the humidity that plagued the town in the late summer was nowhere to be seen.

The café looked like a beautiful nightmare. There was the warm glow of lights, the friendly voices floating through the

Relentless Pursuit

screen door, and the inevitable hours of interrogation she'd face the second she was seen.

"There are many times in life when you just have to suck it up. This is one of those times, dear," Marcy said sweetly as she walked past Tammy with her head held high.

Well, if Marcy could do it, then so could she. Everyone in the cafe converged as soon as Marcy walked through the door. Tammy froze before she got to the door and Nabi stopped behind her. They watched as questions were hurled across the room and people wrapped Marcy in embrace after embrace. It was both sweet and terrifying.

She heard Nabi swallow hard. "I can take you to a secure location if you wish."

"Aw, don't tell me you're scared, Nabi," Tammy cooed. For some reason, his nervousness was what gave her confidence. This wasn't a nightmare. They weren't evil people trying to scare her. These were the people who gave her food when her father was incapacitated. These were the people who cheered for her at graduation. Who gave her an apartment to live in and who took her shopping. These were her friends, no matter if they peppered questions better than any journalist. They cared.

"Um, Miss Fields?" Nabi shook his head as if trying to clear it. "I would swear there is a pig in a pink tutu eating a bowl of salad. Please tell me I am seeing things."

Tammy looked to where Nabi was pointing. Prissy the pig was tied to the lamppost just outside of the cafe. Prissy was dressed in a pink tutu accented with sparkles to match her collar and leash.

"Oh, that's just Prissy. I guess Mr. Tabernacle is here. I should go say hello." Tammy bounded into the café with a renewed energy.

Old Man Tabby sat at the table next to the window so he could keep an eye on Prissy. Townspeople started calling out to Tammy the second she came through the door. She headed straight for Tabby and threw her arms around him in a big hug. His old eyes widened and his face turned pink.

"Thank you for having Prissy protect me. Do you think she can come to the office again tomorrow?"

Tabby's chest puffed with importance as he wiped some crumbs from his overalls. "Of course she can. I'll bring her by in the morning. She's a good pig."

"The best! And she's wearing pink, which is my favorite color! Did you do that just for me?" Tammy teased.

The people nearby snickered and John Wolfe raised a glass of sweet tea. "To Prissy!" The people clapped and Tammy beamed as Tabby burst with pride.

The mood in the café shifted as Prissy became the center of attention. Tammy told her story to Miss Daisy as she sat down at a table with Marcy and Mo. Sensing Tammy wasn't going to last long, Miss Daisy headed straight to the two tables in the center of the room. John and Lily sat back-to-back as they gathered and spread the gossip. By telling them both, Tammy knew everyone in the café would know the story within minutes. She just hoped that they'd hear something from Pierce soon.

The screen door banged closed as Cade and Annie walked in with little Sophie. Marshall and Katelyn followed close behind. Marcy sat up straighter as she watched them approach. "It can't be bad. They're all smiling. Oh, look. There's Will, Kenna, and Sienna. Oh, she's getting so big!" Marcy smiled as the toddler walked into the café with her red curls bouncing as if she owned the place.

"And Morgan and Miles, too." Tammy pointed, her heart lightening as everyone approached the café. Pierce had to be all right. "There's Cole carrying Ryan's carrier with Paige just walking toward the café now. Seems the whole crowd is gathering."

"Hey, Ma!" The boys circled their mother as they took turns kissing her cheek.

"How's Pierce?" Tammy asked. She didn't have Marcy's patience.

Marshall gave her a quick smile. "He'll be here shortly. I dropped him off at the farm to pick up his old Explorer since he can't use the truck anymore."

"It took you this long to do that?" Tammy said as she absent-mindedly tapped her foot.

"No. Noodle called me and told me Dr. Francis wanted to see Pierce to check him out. She might be tiny, but like you, she's a force of nature. So he had to get examined." He held up his hands warding off Tammy's next question. "He's fine. He'll tell you more when he gets here."

Tammy felt relieved and her heart warmed, knowing Emma made Pierce come in just so that she'd feel better. Tammy sat back in her chair and listened as Marcy talked with her daughters-in-law. Cade talked football with Coach Parks and some of the kids on the football team as Annie made her way over to them. Marshall stood by the front door talking with Deputy Dinky and his girlfriend, Chrystal. Annie joined them as she hugged her cousin and teased Dinky about something.

Tammy let their voices and conversation wrap her in safety. She felt her eyes lowering. But she felt a kiss on her cheek just a moment before she would've fallen asleep.

"Oh, Nabi, you shouldn't have," Tammy murmured. Through her lowered lashes, she saw Nabi's eyes go wide from where he stood against the wall.

Pierce chuckled. "So, there was some bonding going on today. Dr. Francis told me all about how she rushed into the lobby and found him lying on top of you." Nabi flushed and looked nervous as Pierce approached him. "Great job. Thanks for saving her. I've kinda grown attached to the little sprite." Pierce held out his hand and Nabi shook it, clearly relieved.

"What happened? Are we safe? Are you hurt?" Tammy fired out before cringing. She sounded just like what she wanted to avoid. "Sorry."

"I'm fine. Dr. Francis said I'm just bumped and bruised. I also told her I was having some snippets of memory coming back. She said when I smell certain things, see something, hear something, or if I'm really tired, then my subconscious triggers the missing memories. They're there, they just need an outlet." Pierce leaned forward and gave her a killer smile. "A kiss will make up for your interrogation," he winked.

"Not in front of your mom!" Tammy whispered as Pierce sat in the chair next to her and picked at the fruit next to Tammy's sandwich with a mischievous glint in his eyes.

"What? Worried you'll be so hot for me you'll just make love right here on the table?" Pierce whispered into her ear, his hot breath caressing the delicate skin of her ear.

She felt on fire just at the suggestion. No, wait, there really was a fire! Pierce's old Ford Explorer was on fire across the street! The explosion came soon after. People gasped as pieces of the SUV rained down.

"Oh my gosh! Pierce, they just blew up your Explorer!" Miss Lily peered out the window at the fiery inferno.

"That's not mine. Mine's parked behind Southern Charms," Pierce said as he wrapped a protective arm around Tammy. He knew it was meant for him, though. They were coming after him.

"Not again!" Coach Parks cried as he pushed past the people crowding the window. He ran out into the street but was stopped by the heat from the fire. He collapsed to his knees. "My baby!" he sobbed.

Pierce sat in the chair next to Tammy as the last of the people inside the café went home. Coach Parks's charred SUV had been towed an hour ago and now Pierce sat with his family and the Rose sisters. They watched as the firemen finished up at the scene.

"I think I have just the thing." Miss Violet patted Pierce on the shoulder and headed for the kitchen. She moved aside a large bag of flour and pulled out a fifth of bourbon. She grabbed a handful of glasses and headed for the tables at the front of the café. "Just for emergencies," Miss Violet said innocently as she started pouring.

Tammy leaned against his chest and sighed. "So, we're still in danger?" she asked even though she already knew the answer. Pierce only squeezed her shoulder and nodded.

His family started talking as Marshall told them of Bridget and the bet. He heard Tammy say how glad she was that Bridget was staying in town for a while, but then the voices swirled into a comforting blanket. Pierce raised the glass of bourbon to his lips and stared off into the night.

"Can I sit here?" the taller man asked. Pierce was no longer at the café. In his mind, he was at the dive bar in downtown Lexington. It wasn't Tammy leaning against him anymore. Instead he felt the man's coat brush against him.

"Sure, man. Whatever." Pierce took another sip of bourbon just as he did that night. His memory was forcing its way to the front of his mind. He saw the man, tall, with trimmed brown hair and a bulbous nose. His face was tan and he had a tattoo peeking out from the top of his white button-down shirt.

"You look like you need a drink." The stranger turned to the bartender and ordered a whole bottle of top-shelf bourbon. "Here, have a glass while I wait for my buddy to get here." The man poured three fingers of bourbon into Pierce's tumbler and half the amount into his. "Cheers!" He lifted the drink and they clicked glasses before shooting the amber liquid.

Pierce smelled the bourbon as he took swallow after swallow of the fine drink. It warmed him slightly and he forgot why he was even there after half a bottle. The man kept filling Pierce's glass over and over.

A shorter man with a thin build appeared and greeted his buddy a little while later. They shook hands and the taller man told him they had a new friend. The little man had wire-rim glasses and a professional look. The two made for an odd couple.

The thin man took the empty seat on the other side of Pierce and started up some small talk. Pierce remembered trying to ask his name, but the little guy started talking football. He asked if anyone in Pierce's family played. Pierce told them about his brothers and growing up in Keeneston. But it didn't last too long. The bottle was almost empty and Pierce was having a hell of a time staying on the barstool.

"Well, gents. It was a pleasure, but I must be getting home." Pierce stumbled off the stool and the large man caught him under the arms and held him up. The little guy rushed over and the two of them propped Pierce up.

"You aren't driving, are you?" the little responsible one asked.

"Nah. Gonna call a cab," Pierce mumbled.

"Hey. We just happen to be heading that way. Let us take you home, buddy. Then you won't have to wait forever for a cab." The men started dragging Pierce out of the bar.

"Thanks, guys. That's real nice of you." Pierce's memory grew fuzzy, but this time he knew why. He had passed out.

Pierce leapt up. Tammy was thrown forward onto the floor and everyone in the café instantly stopped talking and stared at him. His eyes darted around to make sure he was in the present again. "I remembered something! Oh, Tammy! I'm sorry."

"It's okay, what did you remember?" she asked as Pierce helped her off the floor.

"I remember the rest of my time at the bar. I can identify them—and Aiden wasn't lying. It wasn't him or Mrs. Oldham." Pierce told the group of his memory and started pacing the floor as he talked. He knew there was more, he just knew it. Ah! Why couldn't it all come back at once?

Marshall held up the voice recorder on his phone and taped Pierce's recollection. Pierce finished telling them all the details and then looked at them expectantly. "I'll email this over to the detective. I know they'll want you to meet with a sketch artist," Marshall told him as he started punching keys on his phone.

"That's so great, Pierce! I knew you'd remember." Tammy smiled and felt his anxiety level drop. Pierce wrapped her in a hug and kept her there as he rested his chin on the top of her cute little head.

"So, the question still remains—what happened after you got in the car and before Dr. Oldham was killed?" Marshal asked.

Pierce tightened his security hold on Tammy and shook his head. "I don't know, but I *know* there's more. I just feel it!"

"It's okay, honey. You've done a fabulous job. It'll come. Just give it time," Marcy smiled at him in support. He knew she was right. The memories would come on their own when he stopped trying to force it.

"But why didn't they ask about the invention?" Annie said out of nowhere. She cringed. "Sorry, but I just thought that was weird."

"Well, they asked a lot about what I did. Maybe they already knew who I was? I really get the sense I was targeted."

Annie nodded her head. "That's the feeling I get, too. Aiden must've talked. That invention of yours is worth untold millions and someone is out to get it."

"Maybe they were trying to get you to tell them where it was, or where the research papers were so they could claim it just as Aiden and Mrs. Oldham did," Marcy suggested.

"That's not a bad idea, Ma," Cade said as he started to bundle a sleeping Sophie up in the car seat. "We need to get her home. Pierce, let me know if you need anything—anytime, alright?" Cade hugged his brother and waited for Annie to say her good-byes.

Pierce sat on the couch watching as Tammy slipped off her shoes and padded into the bathroom. He enjoyed watching her bedtime routine. She'd get undressed, put her clothes into the laundry basket, wash her face, brush her teeth, and put on those cute little pink pajamas. She was such a contradiction at times. She was all pale pink and softness, yet she never backed down from anything or anyone.

Just as Pierce knew she would, Tammy came out of her room fresh-faced and in her favorite pajamas. She looked utterly delectable. His hands itched to explore every inch of his little nymph.

"Come here," Pierce said huskily as he patted his lap. She smiled and snuggled against him as he wrapped her in his arms. "I love you, sweetheart."

"I love you, too," Tammy said into his chest as the hand that had been resting over his heart started to travel downward over his stomach. He felt his breath hitch as she pulled his shirt from his jeans. "I was so worried today."

"I was, too, sweetheart. I was, too. I don't know what I would've done if you didn't have that vest on." He pushed aside the thin strap of her top, exposing the top of her breast. He gently traced the outline of the large bruise above her heart. "Does it hurt?"

"A little, but I don't notice it unless I'm moving a lot." Tammy's breath caught when Pierce lowered his head and placed a soft kiss on the base of her neck as his hand came up to cup her breast.

"It's a good thing then that I intend to do all the work."

Tammy's head fell back as he started a trail of kisses leading right to "Oh my God!"

CHAPTER TWENTY

A week later, Tammy woke up to knocking on the door. She rolled over expecting to find Pierce, but instead found a note that he'd headed out to the farm to get some work done and that he'd meet her at the café for brunch. Tammy knew who was at the door. She was just surprised Ahmed had knocked.

She got up and pulled on a robe before answering the door. "It's Sunday, couldn't our daily bug sweep have waited another hour? It's practically dark out," she complained as she gladly took the cup of coffee he handed her. He knew she loved the coffee Mo's cook made. He always brought her a large cup to lighten the annoyance of the daily sweep.

Ahmed discovered that her apartment had been bugged the morning after the explosion. It was probably done that morning of the gunfight. Ever since, Ahmed came and swept the apartment for bugs while Bridget ran Marko through every room looking for explosives.

True to their word, the Rose sisters and John hadn't allowed anyone to pass through town without being identified. They obtained copies of the sketches Pierce made with the police and had farmers operating as spies, checking out drivers as they worked the fields along the roadways. They diligently called in anyone remotely resembling the pictures. Further, Tabby left Prissy at the office every morning to guard the back door. Nabi took up residence outside the front of the office looking every bit a deadly statue.

Sadly, she'd gotten used to Dinky, Noodle, Nabi, and others from Ahmed's security force following her. They tagged along to the movies with her and Pierce and followed close behind when they went on a horseback-and-picnic date out at the farm. It turned out that she and Pierce had similar simple tastes. They preferred low-key dates where they held hands and spent time out in the warm summer air.

Memorial Day had been perfect. All the veterans in town paraded down Main Street in their uniforms led by the high school marching band. Main Street was then shut down as townspeople unloaded grills, smokers, and casserole dishes for a large cookout. Kids ran around and played with Prissy the Pig. She and Pierce had spent the day with friends and family and, most importantly, with each other.

"The apartment's clean. I'll see you tomorrow," Ahmed said preparing to leave.

"You sure are a man of few words. You know, maybe if you talked a little more with that sexy accent, you might find a date or two," Tammy teased.

"Who says I haven't already had a date or two?" Ahmed turned and walked out leaving Tammy with her mouth slightly open. What else had Ahmed been up to? Well, she was likely never to find out.

She walked across her apartment and pulled off her pajamas. She was feeling good today. Nothing had happened in a week and maybe they were just going to be left alone. For some reason she felt that today started a new chapter in her life. She pulled out her jean shorts and a pink peasant top. She ran a flat iron through her growing blonde hair and slipped into her cowboy boots before hurrying out the door.

Tammy knew something was wrong the second she opened the café's kitchen door. Miss Violet was standing with her hands on her plump hips staring out into the restaurant. Women's voices floated through the air and Tammy cringed. One of those voices belonged to Kandi Chase Rawlings. Tammy took a deep breath. She wouldn't let anyone ruin what started as an excellent day.

"What's going on?" Tammy asked Miss Violet who jumped in surprise.

"Lordy, you scared me. You might want to go back upstairs for a little while," Miss Violet said nervously as she tried to block Tammy's view of the patrons.

"I know, Kandi's a real…" Tammy paused and tried to think of a nice way to say it. "Well, bless her little heart, but she's a horrible person. I can handle it."

Tammy stood on her tiptoes and peeked over Miss Violet's head and decided that maybe she couldn't handle it. She saw Kandi and Jasmine sitting on either side of Pierce at the table closest to Miss Violet's window. Pierce had his back to her and both the girls had their blown-up breasts pushed against him as their hands ran all over him.

"You poor dear! So, you've dipped your toe on the other side of the tracks… or trailer park in this case. You must be so bored with that trashy little mite! What would you call her, Jas?" Kandi laughed as she leaned across Pierce to wink at Jasmine.

"I don't know, Kandi, but certainly not a woman! She doesn't have the required parts that I know Pierce enjoys so much." Tammy looked down at her chest and then to theirs. They were right. She was nowhere near as inflated. But what worried her was the way Pierce just sat there not saying a thing.

Miss Violet's arm came around Tammy's waist as she felt her eyes tear up when Jasmine offered to come over to see him tonight. Suddenly a woman standing up at the table nearby drew Tammy's attention. She watched in stunned silence as Neely Grace got up from the table she shared with Henry and stood in front of Jasmine.

If Neely Grace or Henry saw Tammy standing in the kitchen, then she didn't know. Neely Grace had been stopping by Keeneston a lot more and Tammy was so embarrassed that her new friend would hear such horrible things about her. Neely Grace probably said those things about her in high school, but over the past weeks she'd been nothing but the nicest of women.

"You're the president of the Keeneston Belles, aren't you?" Neely Grace asked with such sweetness and admiration that Tammy's heart dropped. Neely Grace was reverting.

"Why, yes, I am." Jasmine held her head high with that pride.

"Now, forgive me, I've been gone for a while, but what is the motto of the Belles?" Neely Graced waved a perfectly manicured hand in the air. "Oh, not the husband-catching part, the one that's actually written down," she said with a sweet smile.

"A Belle is to serve our community with grace, dignity, poise, and politeness. We are the shining beacon of all that is womanly and good in Keeneston," Jas said with a smile and Tammy suddenly felt like throwing up.

"Then, may I ask, why is the head of such a great organization over here acting like a strumpet?" Neely Grace asked with an innocent smile.

Tammy and Miss Violet both gasped in surprise as Jasmine started to thank Neely Grace before realizing she'd just been insulted. "Excuse me! You have no right to talk to me like that, you uptight..."

"Belle. I'm an uptight Belle. Neely Grace Sinclair, actually. And my great-, great-, great-grandmother was one of the founders of the Belles. As such, I and my family hold lifetime membership and are unable to be expelled except in cases of egregious circumstances. However, if pursuant to a vote of the current Belles, we find that you are not up to par with our motto, we may cancel your membership at any time. Isn't that right?"

Jasmine sputtered as Neely Grace stood quietly with a smile on her face watching Jasmine trying to think of what to say. "I call a vote!" Mary Alice Duke called from her table.

"And I second," Neely Grace said with every ounce of quiet power behind her voice.

Mary Alice clapped her hands and gave Neely Grace a hug. "It's so good to have you back! I'll call the meeting together!" Before Jasmine could argue, Neely Grace looked up and gave Tammy a wink before heading back to a proud and beaming Henry.

Pierce finally turned his head and saw Tammy standing there. His eyes went wide and his face paled. Tammy narrowed her eyes and left the kitchen as fast as she could. She was too angry to talk and she was certainly too angry to say anything to Pierce.

Nabi was on duty this morning and emerged from his car in the parking lot when he saw her hurrying out as Pierce called after her.

"We're leaving now. Right now." Tammy hurried to where Nabi had jumped to open the door.

"Aren't we waiting for Mr. Davies?"

"Certainly not. And right now I wouldn't feel too bad if you ran over his foot." She slid into the car and didn't even look back as Nabi left Pierce in a cloud of dust.

***

Pierce tossed a chip onto the table and waited for his brothers to make their bets. He glared at Ahmed sitting across from him as he tossed in another bet. Tammy hadn't spoken to him all day. In fact, she had been at Mo's with Ahmed or mini-Ahmed playing bodyguard to her.

"I'm surprised you came tonight," Pierce sneered as he narrowed his eyes at Ahmed.

"Why? I always make it to the weekly poker game," Ahmed said calmly as he caught Mo out of the corner of his eye tossing in his cards and heading for the kitchen in Pierce's temporary apartment above Southern Charms.

"Did I miss something when I was gone on my honeymoon?" Miles asked as he looked around the table. He looked tanned and relaxed from the week he and Morgan spent on the beach at Saint Barts.

"Nah. Pierce here just put his foot in his mouth—or rather, he put a hand over his mouth and didn't say a word," Marshall laughed.

"Shut up, Marsh," Pierce snapped as the others chuckled. Miles looked between Pierce and Marshall as his brow furrowed in confusion.

"See, Pierce here got ambushed by the bimbo duo of Kandi and Jasmine, who proceeded to bad-mouth Tammy up one side and down the other. But, little brother here didn't say a word. It was Neely Grace who finally took the matter in hand. And I'll give you one guess as to who saw the whole thing," Marshall told them with a smile on his face.

"Why didn't you say anything? You always stick up for people?" Miles asked.

"I didn't want to get into a big blow-up in the middle of the café. I was afraid if I started in on them, then I wouldn't stop," Pierce explained as he ran a hand over his face. "Is Tammy still at your place?" Pierce asked Mo.

"No. Nabi took her home a while ago," Mo said casually as he was poured himself and Will a drink.

"I'm guessing you're in such a mood because you realize Tammy isn't one of those women who will just shrug it off for a chance to be with you. She's more like Paige. I still haven't heard the end of giving her a vacuum as a gift. The other day she even admitted that it picked up Chuck hair as she gave me the evil eye." Cole shook his head as he tossed in a chip. "But it makes marriage worth it. It's never boring. With loyalty and passion like that, you know you have a lifetime together ahead of you."

"Now I think we're getting somewhere," Cade said with a grin.

"I agree, brother. I think he's just realized how badly he messed up," Marshall told the group. "See that look right there? That's the look of a man who just realized he screwed up big time with the woman he wants to marry."

Pierce shot up from his seat and stared down at his brother. "I didn't say anything about marriage!"

"You didn't need to. We've all looked in the mirror and seen that same face," Marshall laughed. "You just better make up with her before Cy gets home or he might just…"

Pierce had had it! His blood pressure had been steadily climbing all day. He was angry with Ahmed for playing big brother and hiding Tammy all day. He was angry with Marshall for his constant teasing. But as Pierce launched himself over the table connecting his fist with Marshall's face, he realized he was mostly angry with himself for messing up the best thing he had in his life.

Marshall grabbed him and tossed him to the floor. When Cade and Miles tried to break it up, they got drawn into it. Marshall punched Cade by accident and, in retaliation, Cade tackled Marshall to the ground. Miles tried to pick Pierce up and accidently hit him with an elbow. Then it was just a free-for-all. All they were missing was Cy jumping on their backs and Paige shooting them with her slingshot.

Marcy Davies carried a large basket of food up the stairs to Pierce's apartment. She opened the door and was transported back in time fifteen years to see her sons rolling around on the floor in an all-out brawl. She set the basket of food down on the kitchen island where Mo, Will, and Cole stood watching the melee.

"Will, Mo, Cole, how are you doing tonight?"

"Fine, ma'am. Thanks for asking. My mother was just wondering when she'd get to see you again." Will smiled and she couldn't help but return it.

"That's so nice of them. I'll call Betsy tomorrow," Marcy said as she pulled out the length of the hose from the faucet.

"Lovely evening, Mrs. Davies. Do you require any assistance?" Mo asked curiously.

Marcy turned on the water and took a couple steps toward the rolling mountain made up of her sons. "To break up a fight? Goodness no!" Marcy smiled as she sprayed the water across the island and onto her boys. They shouted and immediately jumped up sputtering. "Good evening, boys. I brought you some dinner."

She enjoyed herself as her tall, strapping sons all standing and shuffling their feet in embarrassment for getting caught by their mother. They all murmured a hello to her.

Marcy looked around. "Where's Ahmed? I'm surprised he didn't stop this the second it started."

"This was between brothers and he went to check on Tammy," Mo told them with a playful grin on his face.

All of her sons turned and looked at Pierce and she started to understand what started this fight. When she saw his face turn red and heard Pierce curse under his breath, she knew for sure what it was. Oh, it wouldn't be that much longer! She couldn't wait to get home to tell Jake.

Pierce kissed his mother on her cheek and thanked her for dinner. He slipped out the door as Marcy started serving dinner for everyone before she headed home. Pierce didn't need to tell them where he was going. They'd figure it out and probably tease him some more. But it was worth it.

Pierce ran down the street and up the back staircase to Tammy's apartment. He stopped himself from knocking to try to straighten up. He tucked in his shirt and wiped the little bit of blood from his lip off on the back of his hand before knocking.

Ahmed answered the door and Pierce reined in his temper. "What are you doing here?"

"I came to check in for the evening before leaving the night shift outside." Ahmed opened the door wider and Pierce walked in.

"What are you doing here? Did Jasmine leave you all warm and satisfied so you thought you'd come see if your trailer trash girlfriend who put herself out there to protect you is still alive?" Tammy shot at him. "Oh my gosh! What happened to your face?"

Pierce felt a sense of relief he had never known before wash over him as she hurried to look at the cut on his lip. "It's nothing. My brothers were just teaching me to be less of an ass."

"I'd like to hear more about that, but first let me get something for your lip."

Pierce watched as Tammy went into the little kitchen to search through her freezer. She went up on her tiptoes and the hem of her short robe raised up to show she was wearing some very new pink and black underwear. Silk from the looks of it. Pierce whipped his head around and saw Ahmed still standing there.

"Don't worry. If I didn't do anything when she was naked in the shower, then I won't do anything now. Besides, I just spent the last ten minutes convincing her that silence can be golden. Good luck. Remember, if you don't fix this, I'll kill you."

Pierce smiled. "Thank you. I think it's best that I don't ask about the shower," Ahmed started to slip out the door when Pierce stopped him. "You wouldn't really kill me, would you?" Ahmed just looked at him for a moment and then left. Pierce was pretty sure that meant no.

"Here you go," Tammy took his hand and led him over to the couch. She leaned over and held the bag of frozen peas to his lip.

"Tammy, I'm so sorry. I should've stopped them. I was just so angry I was afraid I wouldn't be able to control my temper. What I was thinking of calling them was a lot worse than what Neely Grace said. Although, I think what she did will have greater impact than me giving them a piece of my mind. Will you ever forgive me?"

"I already did. Now, I won't lie. I thought about some very bad things, but Ahmed told me how some men handle conflict quietly and that one of his men overheard a rant you gave yourself in the parking lot after I left," Tammy told him.

"You, and only you, are who I think of day and night. You are the woman I want to have in my bed." He traced his fingers down her throat and to the *V* her robe created and Tammy felt her breath quicken. "Did you and your Greek ever talk about marriage?"

Tammy stood up from where she was holding the peas against his face. "No. We only dated a few weeks. Why?"

"Just wondering. So, time is important to you then?" Pierce hedged.

Tammy felt her heart pounding. She felt lightheaded. Was he asking her what she thought he was? "Time is irrelevant when you're with the right man." She held her breath as Pierce seemed lost in thought for a moment.

"Am I the right man, Tammy?"

"You'll have to ask to find out." Tammy mentally chanted "Oh my God, Oh my God" as she waited to see what Pierce would do next. She wasn't completely prepared for him to simply nod and accept what she said as he looked up at her with such burning passion that she thought she'd melt on the spot.

Pierce ran his hands up her legs until his hands grasped her bottom and pulled her near. She straddled his leg as he pulled her astride. He leaned back against the couch and silently untied her robe to let it fall open. He only stared for a moment. Then his hands claimed her. "I think I'm that man," he murmured the moment before he took her.

CHAPTER TWENTY-ONE

Pierce slowly pulled his arm out from under Tammy's head in the early morning hours. They had made love over and over again last night. Most of the time they hadn't said a word, just looking each other in the eyes and conveying all the love they felt in their actions.

Pierce rolled out of bed as Tammy shifted uneasily in her sleep. He quietly whistled for Marko to take his place in bed. Tammy threw her arm over Marko and settled back into peaceful sleep. Pierce slid into his clothes and quietly walked out of the apartment, leaving Tammy sound asleep in bed.

He ran down the street, looking behind him every couple of steps. The sun was just rising and he'd be able to see if he was being followed. The town seemed to be just waking up this Monday morning. He could hear the cows mooing in the distance as farmers started their rounds. The Rose sisters would be unlocking the doors to the café soon.

He picked up his pace, hoping no one would see him as he ducked down the side road and stopped in front of the house he sought. He raised his hand and knocked softly knowing they'd be up. The door opened and Cole stood with his cowboy hat on looking as if he were getting ready to drive into Lexington for work.

"Morning, Cole. I need to see my sister. Please tell me she hasn't left yet."

Paige hurried to the door and looked out before Cole even had a chance to call her. "Pierce, what's the matter?"

"I need your help."

Tammy snagged a couple pieces of bacon from Miss Violet before walking to work. Bridget had picked up Marko just a moment ago and they had ended up talking about getting something for Tammy in terms of personal protection. While Tammy felt comfortable with a gun, she decided it wasn't her thing, but the cute pink bottle of pepper spray was.

She took a bite of the bacon as she enjoyed the bustle of the morning. Her heels clicked on the sidewalk as Tammy enjoyed the sense of being part of the morning rituals of the town. Lawyers were heading to court, shops were opening, and she had had the most magical night of her life. She did have to admit that she was disappointed when she woke up snuggling Marko instead of Pierce. But she knew Pierce's occupation and it required many early morning starts. Tammy just couldn't wait to see him for lunch.

Tammy unlocked the front door to the law office and knew that Henry, Kenna, and Dani would already be at court. She turned on the lights and opened the curtains to let the sun in. She walked past her desk and into the kitchen in the back. Tammy started the coffee pot so it would be ready when she finished the great cup left by Ahmed.

The phone rang and she hurried to her desk to answer it. "Rooney Law Office," she practically sang into the phone. "Hi, Mr. Tabernacle! No, I understand. It's very important for Prissy to be groomed. How about she takes the day off?" Tammy giggled to herself as she hung up the phone and finally sat down to turn on her computer.

She heard a beep before she could bend down to push the button on her computer. Tammy looked around but didn't see where it could've come from. Oh well, she bent down and was about to press the button on her CPU sitting on the floor when she saw a red glow reflecting off the computer.

Tammy shrugged and turned on the computer. As she sat back up, she knocked the Sanderson file to the ground. Notes spilled out and Tammy let out a puff of air in annoyance as she bent back over to pick it up. She gathered it up and then reached under her chair for the last piece of paper. That's when she saw it. She was bent to the side and could see the red light coming from the bottom of her office chair.

Tammy gulped. She didn't know what it was, but it couldn't be good. She straightened up as fear paralyzed her. The door opened and she looked in fear as a person entered. She swallowed hard, terrified to even say a word as she watched Bridget walk happily into the office.

"Hey, Tammy! I got you that pepper spray we talked about," Bridget said as Marko's head shot up sniffing the air. Marko pulled hard on the leash. Bridget let go, thinking he wanted to see Tammy. Marko sniffed some more and barked excitedly as he ran over to Tammy and sat down, his eyes never leaving the chair Tammy was sitting on. "Oh crap," Bridget whispered as she called Marko off the positive indication for explosives.

"Is it a bomb?" Tammy whispered.

"Hold on and I'll tell you. Just don't move." Bridget walked close to Tammy and then crawled under her chair on her back to take a look. "Um, yeah, it's a bomb. A nasty one, too. It's on a pressure sensor. If you stand up, it'll go off."

Tammy fought the instinct to run. She took a couple deep breaths and waited for Bridget to finish her inspection of the bomb. "Is it something you can turn off?"

"No. This is very intricate and there are even false leads here. It may look like the right wire to cut but could mean instant detonation. I have an Air Force buddy on the bomb squad. He'll know who to call." Bridget crawled back out and stood up. "Let me take Marko to the car and I'll be right back."

Tammy waited impatiently for Bridget and gave a sigh of relief when she heard the door open. Only it wasn't Bridget, it was Miss Lily. "Miss Lily! You gotta leave, right now!" Tammy whispered.

She knew the bomb wouldn't go off, but she felt it didn't need any surprises to scare it either.

"What, dear? I can't hear you," Miss Lily said with a happy smile on her face as she walked further into the office.

"You need to leave now! It's not safe." Tammy raised her voice and saw that Miss Lily finally heard her.

"Oh, pish-posh. Your men are right outside talking with Bridget. We're perfectly safe. I can't say the same about Jasmine, though."

"Miss Lily, there is a bomb under my chair that could go off at any minute! You need to leave right now!" Tammy felt the tears start to roll down her face. She didn't want to die and she certainly didn't want to kill anyone else if she did go.

"A bomb! Goodness gracious!" Miss Lily was clearly shocked, but then she smiled. "Does John know? Of course he doesn't. If he did, everyone in town would be here! I got the scoop and I'm going to feed it to that old goat!" Miss Lily pulled out her cell phone and placed the first call to the café, the second to her neighbor, Edna, and the last to Pam Gilbert.

"Miss Lily, there's a good chance I'm going to die. Why don't you just drop this act and admit you like Mr. Wolfe?"

"I can't have him thinking I'm loose. He stole two kisses from me and I intend to make him work for the third." Then Miss Lily just waved her hand in the air. "And you're not going to die. You have the best of the best on their way. They'll find a way to disarm it. Now, do you want to hear about Jasmine?"

Miss Lily clearly wasn't afraid of the bomb. She pulled up a chair and took a seat as they waited for the rush of people to come. Tammy was guessing they had less than a minute before the first group arrived.

"Sure, why not? I'm not going anywhere." Tammy exhaled and just hoped the bomb wasn't set off by gossip.

"Well, Neely Grace and Mary Alice called a meeting of the Belles and they kicked Jasmine out! Now, we weren't privy to all of what was said, but apparently it was very heated. Jasmine stormed out and rumor has it she was seen being dropped off at her house by one Detective Cowell last night. But, what else is interesting is that

Neely Grace was elected president of the Belles and they've already started to change their ways. Why, it was announced just yesterday at church that they were holding a bake sale to raise money to send care packages to all the deployed soldiers from Keeneston."

Before Tammy could tell Miss Lily how much she liked Neely Grace, they heard what sounded like a body hitting the door. Nabi was plastered against the door trying to keep out what looked to be the whole café.

"And, it seems that Neely Grace and Henry are going strong, although I don't know if I'd want to be in a family with Martha. I mean, you know how much of a stickler she is at the D.A.'s office. Can you imagine Sunday dinner?" Miss Lily shuddered and ignored the mob of gossipers currently trying to pry Nabi from the door.

"Do you think you should go help him?" Tammy nodded to the door where Miss Violet was hitting Nabi with her wooden spoon.

"Nah. They'll get in soon enough. So, did Pierce make up for yesterday?" Miss Lily continued completely indifferent to the near-riot occurring outdoors.

Because this could be the last conversation she might have, she might as well enjoy it. "Yes. He was really sweet and apologized. Then we had mind-blowing sex." If Miss Lily could be so nonchalant, then so could she. However, she was really disappointed when Miss Lily didn't flutter about in shock.

"I bet. Make-up sex is always the best," she said with a nod of her white head.

"Miss Lily!"

"What? I was young once, too, you know," Miss Lily said with a shrug.

"What are you talking about? You're still young," Henry said as he walked in from the back.

"Where did you come from?" Miss Lily asked as she looked from Henry to where Edna was pointing a huge gun at Nabi to try to force him to move.

"I used the back door. I guess no one thought of that. So, you're sitting on a bomb? Don't think you're getting workers' comp for this," Henry joked as he pulled up another seat.

"Ha-ha. I could just cash in all my vacation time considering I've never taken more than a day here and there for five years. You owe me for almost a year by now." Tammy took a breath and tried to stay light-hearted, but it wasn't working. She was literally sitting on death. "I guess I can't convince you and Miss Lily to leave."

"Nope. Bridget, Marshall, Ahmed, and Annie have quietly left the deputies and Mo's men out front and made their way to the back. They're talking with bomb experts and I'm to tell you that some Air Force guy in the explosive ordinance disposal unit is flying in and will meet with the Lexington and Kentucky State Police bomb squads. Those guys all know each other and then they'll come up with a plan of action." Henry leaned back in his chair and calmly crossed his ankles as he stretched out his legs.

"How long will that take?" Tammy was trying not to get nervous. If it meant her life, then she'd sit here forever.

"Lexington Bomb Squad will be here in about ten minutes. State police in about twenty and the specialist was down at the 101st Airborne giving a talk. They're flying up in a Blackhawk and landing at Mo's farm in about…" Henry looked at his watch, "…twenty-five minutes. Hang in there. We'll have you out in time for lunch."

"Has anyone called Pierce?"

"We can't get an answer. Marshall put an A.P.B. on him and he'll be here soon," Henry said with a smile she knew was fake. At least he wasn't as unaffected as she thought. They were just really good actors and friends. While Tammy worried about their safety, she didn't know what she would've done if she didn't have Miss Lily there to get the scoop on Henry and his new girlfriend. She'd have to find some way to thank them, because they were the only reason she was able to remain calm.

Pierce sat in the passenger's seat of Paige's truck and knew something was wrong the instant they arrived in town. The streets were packed with people. No one was inside. They were all walking toward downtown, but a barricade stopped them as they tried to drive to Southern Charms. Noodle came racing out to them waving his arms and screaming into his radio.

"Thank goodness! Where have you been? Answer your phone, man!" Noodle yelled as Pierce jumped out of the truck. He pulled out his phone and saw he had twenty-three missed calls and his heart stopped beating.

"Tammy?" He barely got out.

"Alive for now. She's sitting on a live bomb at the office. Bomb squads from all around the state are here. They're just now setting up. You better hurry!"

Pierce took off at a dead run. The people in the streets saw him coming and moved out of the way as they headed to the troopers' barricade to see what was happening. Pierce was stopped by a state trooper and thought he'd punch the guy as he explained who he was.

"Let him through!" Bridget yelled from the doorway of the office. Pierce sprinted the remaining fifty yards and stopped as Bridget, Miles, and Ahmed stepped forward to keep him out of the office.

"Is Tammy going to be okay?" he asked again as he tried to see her.

"She's being briefed. Look, Pierce, the three of us have looked at the device before the bomb squads got here. If we're right, then there's a secondary trigger that will blow within seconds of the main wire being cut." Miles put his hand on Pierce's shoulder and made him look at him. "Do you understand what I'm saying?"

"That no matter what, it's going to blow?" Pierce fought the urge to hyperventilate. He took a deep breath and tried not to break down.

"Is this him?" a man who looked like he belonged on Wall Street instead of in the large bomb suit asked as he came to stand next to Bridget.

"Yup. Pierce, this is Sergeant Webber from the Air Force EOD division. What did you find?" Bridget asked.

"It's what you thought. But I think we may be able to fool it long enough to get her off," Sergeant Webber said with a grin that exposed two dimples.

"What do you mean?" Pierce asked as he got a look of a white-faced Tammy talking to another member of the squad.

"Well, it appears the sensor is for a range of weight. Men don't know how to guess women's weight, so they usually use a range. It doesn't hurt anything to add weight. It's when you stand up that the lack of pressure triggers the bomb. So, we're going to add weight as we bring her off of it. Bomb blankets are incredibly heavy and they may work to contain the blast some. I have a bomb suit I'm borrowing from the Lexington Bomb Squad and so does the state police. My idea is to move her to the parking lot. Her chair has wheels and it shouldn't be a problem. It'll reduce the risk of property damage and human casualty. Jamison there will get into the dumpster with two blankets and whatever else heavy we can find. He'll lower those blankets onto the chair from the dumpster at the same time I pull her slowly off and behind the blast wall we're setting up."

"You've got to be joking! That's the best you can do? Can't you disarm it?" Pierce said in a state between absolute fear and anger.

"No. This is a very sophisticated bomb and sometimes it just takes a simple plan. One way or another, this bomb is detonating. I'm just hoping I can confuse it long enough to get her out of the way. Now she's waiting for you. Go see her while I work out the details."

Pierce knew he was being dismissed, but he didn't care. All he wanted was Tammy. Detective Basher stood by quietly as the Kentucky State Trooper Jamison finished explaining the game plan. He could tell that Tammy didn't quite believe him as her eyes kept growing wider and wider as he talked to her.

Detective Basher was the first one to see him and gently put his hand on Tammy's shoulder to draw her attention to Pierce while reminding her to keep seated. Tears started flowing the second she saw him and she had to bite her lip to keep from sobbing.

"Sweetheart, it's okay. I'm here." Pierce sat on his knees in front of her and grabbed her hands in his. He brought them up to his face and kissed them as he hung tight to her.

"Oh, Pierce! I'm so sorry," she cried. Detective Basher and Jamison looked at each other and took a couple steps away to give them some privacy.

"Tammy, you don't have anything to be sorry for. I'm the one who has regrets. I regret I didn't say anything to those two evil women yesterday, and I regret I didn't let myself fall in love with you two years ago. But I love you now so much and nothing is going to change that. These guys are going to save you. They have a great plan. You just need to listen to them and do exactly what they say. Then we can begin to live our lives with no regrets."

Pierce had to choke back the tears that were threatening to come out. He took in every detail of her—the way her hair fell across her face, her cute nose, the softness of her hands—and prayed it wouldn't be the last time he looked at her.

He turned his head to try to get himself under control and saw Jamison and Sergeant Webber coming toward them. His time was up. How could he tell her all he wanted to in mere seconds?

"It's time, sweetheart. You're the strongest woman I know. You're a survivor and you will survive this, too. I will always love you. Always." Pierce felt the tears come, but he didn't care. He stood up and placed his lips on hers in one last gentle kiss. "I'll see you in a couple minutes, okay?"

Tammy tried to smile. "Okay," she said softly. Basher started to clear the area while Jamison and Webber put the rest of their suits on. "Pierce, I love you too."

Detective Basher came and put his arm around Pierce's shoulder and gently pulled him away. "Come on. They have a truck we can watch the live feed from. Both the guys have cameras on their heads. You'll be with her every step of the way."

Pierce nodded but stopped at the door. He had to have one last look at her. She was looking up at the two men in the bomb suits as they got ready to start pushing her outside. The tears had stopped and pure perseverance was etched across her beautiful face. He'd remember it always.

CHAPTER TWENTY-TWO

Tammy closed her eyes as Pierce walked out of the office. She didn't think she could stand watching him leave. She was near panic as it was and to think that it was the last time she'd see him would send her over the edge. Sergeant Webber's voice brought her back through.

"Ma'am, I need you to open your eyes." Tammy opened her eyes and looked into Webber's face—at least, the part that wasn't covered by a huge collar and helmet. "Good. Now, I am not going to let you die. Do you understand that?"

Tammy looked at him again and saw that he truly believed it and it gave her hope. "Yes. I do."

"Excellent. We're going to hold onto the chair on its back and on the armrests. I need you to lean back and grasp the edges here as hard as you can." Webber waited for her to follow his instructions before he nodded to Jamison to grab the chair. "Now you're just going for a little ride."

Tammy held her breath as they started rolling slowly across the carpeted floor. The further across the room they got, the worse she became. She was afraid her grip would loosen or they'd hit a bump.

"So while we're just hanging out. I have a question for you, ma'am."

Tammy looked into Jamison's dark face and saw a hint of humor in his brown eyes.

"Yes?" Tammy asked, unsure really how to handle a question at a time like this.

"Who is that woman out there with the huge knockers fawning over all the officers?"

Tammy broke out laughing. She didn't need any further description because one woman truly fit that description. "That's Kandi." She laughed again when she saw the huge smiles on their faces. "Figures you all would notice her." Tammy rolled her eyes at the typical guy behavior.

"It's pretty hard not to when she purposely runs the barricade just to have an officer escort her out… four times. Maybe you can settle our bet then. See, I bet Webber here that she's a stripper at Big Bunny's in Lexington."

"And," Webber jumped in, "I bet she's a three-time divorcée looking for husband number four."

"So, which one of us won?" Jamison asked with the nicest smile that had Tammy giggling as she was moved down the hall toward the back door.

"Neither. She's a married soccer mom."

"Poor bastard," Jamison said as Webber nodded in agreement.

"But if I had to pick someone to date, it wouldn't be her. What kind of men did you take us for?" Jamison joked.

"Um, typical?" Tammy teased.

"Ouch. See, I'd have chosen you if you weren't already taken," Webber winked and they rolled her through the open door.

"Nah, I'd have taken Granny with the Smith and Wesson. Any woman who carries a gun like that is a keeper," Jamison laughed.

Tammy took a deep breath and realized they had reached their destination. The guys had successfully kept her distracted as they transported her. Just having that over with was enough to bolster her confidence.

She looked around the tiny parking lot and saw that all the cars had been moved. A couple of boards had been put up to cover the nearest windows. In the middle of the lot stood the large metal dumpster and what looked like a clear dressing screen.

"You ready to do this?" Webber asked as he positioned her against the dumpster.

Tammy took a breath and nodded. "I am. I have a date to go on tonight."

Jamison chuckled as he let go and climbed the stairs that had been placed beside the dumpster as Webber wedged the bottom of the chair in place and then draped a bomb blanket around the three sides, leaving the leg area uncovered.

"This is to help contain the explosion. Jamison there has a bomb blanket against the inner wall of the dumpster as well. So we'll be safe. Now it's you we need to work on." Webber attached a collar and helmet to her as he explained it wasn't nearly as thick as the ones they were wearing, but it would be enough to help her. He attached a bulletproof vest as well before checking on Jamison.

"Okay, we're good to go. Now, Jamison is going to be behind and above you. He's going to lower that sandbag there. It's very heavy. When you feel it being wedged behind you, you need to start scooting forward in your chair. Don't get off. Just scoot forward until you're on the edge of the seat. Got it?" Webber asked.

"Got it. What then?"

"Then I'm going to count to three and pull while you jump. Don't go for distance, just jump right into my arms, okay. Pretend I'm that boyfriend of yours. You leap into my arms, I'll catch you, and then I'm going to dive behind the blast wall. I'll land on top of you. Since you're so tiny, I'll be able to completely cover you, keeping you safe. Don't panic, because I'll probably knock the air out of you. Just know it'll come back. At the same time, Jamison is going to drop our last bomb blanket over the chair in hopes of further containment and dive into the dumpster."

"Oh, is that all? A perfectly orchestrated pound-for-pound exchange and then just jump to safety?" Tammy felt the panic start roaring to the surface.

"Yes. That's it. A simple exchange of weight. The device will need to recalibrate the weight to determine if it should explode. That will give us the second we need to get behind the wall."

"A second? That's all?" Tammy tried to take a deep breath and calm herself.

"A second was all I needed to fall in love with you," Webber winked.

Tammy rolled her eyes before she could even stop herself and all the nervousness bubbled out as laughter. "Do you know my boss?"

"If you're done flirting, we're ready to go," Jamison called from where he stood above Tammy with a large sandbag.

"Ready?" Webber asked her as he looked her right into the eyes.

"Let's do this!" Tammy said as her anxiety peaked.

Webber took a step back so that he was slightly behind the blast wall, widened his stance, and opened his arms. Jamison slowly lowered the sandbag onto the seat behind her. Tammy held her breath and slowly inched forward as the bag pressed further and further down on her back.

Soon the bag was sitting fully on the seat and she was sitting on the edge. The whole time she hadn't taken her eyes off of Jamison. He held up one finger. It was Go Time. Two. Deep Breath. Three. Tammy closed her eyes and thought of Pierce as she launched herself forward.

Pierce stood in the police truck watching the steady progress down the hall. Henry stood next to him in his customary shiny suit and continually moved from one foot to another as they listened to the discussion between Jamison and Webber. He strained to hear Tammy's voice, but it was too muffled through the bomb suits.

Ahmed snuck into the truck and stood quietly as they all continued to watch. The bomb squad commander was giving directions every now and then, but Pierce didn't hear them. He just kept his eyes glued to where Tammy sat. He felt Henry laugh next to him when Webber laid his one-liner on Tammy and saw the way Tammy relaxed a little. He'd never been so thankful for someone to hit on his girlfriend.

Pierce lost his breath, though, when he heard Webber start the countdown. He dared himself not to blink as Tammy launched herself into the air. Webber reached out and snatched her right out of the air. He tucked her tight against him and dove for the blast wall. Pierce saw them hit the ground hard, but then the cameras went dark. The truck rocked and car alarms went off all down the street.

Not waiting for the smoke to clear, Pierce shoved his way out of the truck and knocked an officer to the ground who tried to prevent him from entering the office. The abandoned office seemed so surreal as he ran down the back hall and shoved the door open. The heat pushed him back for a second as the smoke instantly clung to him. A tree was ablaze and pieces of debris lay scattered.

"Where are they?" Ahmed called as he ran to Pierce with Henry right behind.

Pierce looked around and as the smoke cleared, he saw Webber in his bomb suit on the ground to the right. "There!"

The men pushed forward through the smoke as the sirens from the fire trucks and first responders entered the barricaded area. Pierce dropped to the ground beside Webber and tried to push him off to get to Tammy. Webber fought to untangle himself, but Henry and Ahmed each grabbed an arm and pulled him up. Tammy lay motionless on the ground with her eyes squeezed shut.

"Tammy!" Pierce yelled, but she didn't respond.

"She probably can't hear you because of the explosion and the adrenaline," Ahmed said as both he and Henry quickly forgot about Webber and knelt beside her.

Pierce grabbed her then and pulled her to him. Her eyes shot open and Pierce was overcome with joy. She was alive! He watched as a huge grin covered her face. Ahmed and Henry leaned forward and hugged her as he just savored having her in his arms.

"Henry! You've ruined your favorite suit?" Tammy laughed as she clung to Pierce.

"It's okay. I was thinking of getting some new ones anyway. There was this great pinstripe I saw when I was out with Neely Grace the other night."

Tammy laughed again. Neely Grace had managed in one week to get rid of the shiny suits. She was her hero! Tammy looked to see two firemen rushing to help Jamison out of the dumpster. He saw her and gave her a thumps-up. Ahmed stood up and helped Webber get out of his suit as Jamison made his way over.

"Damn, girl! You did great!" Turning to shake Pierce's hand, Jamison said, "You are one lucky man, if I may say so."

"You did perfect. I'm going to talk to the bomb squad. I'll see you in a minute, okay?" Webber asked as Tammy nodded with the thanks she didn't know how to express in her eyes.

Ahmed and Henry went with him to let everyone know she was all right and he finally got to have her all to himself for just a moment. Pierce pulled her into his lap and kissed her with everything he had.

"You were so brave," Pierce said in between kisses.

"I was, wasn't I?" Tammy laughed. "I'm sorry, I'm just so happy to be alive. Oh, Pierce, all I wanted was to get back to you. I love you so much."

"I love you too, sweetheart." He lowered his head and kissed her again while the parking lot filled with people.

Tammy sat on the edge of the ambulance as Dr. Francis and the EMTs examined her. Noodle had called Emma when he found out about the situation and she'd left work to make sure Tammy was well cared for.

"You've had a tough couple of weeks. You're remarkably lucky. You have some cuts and I'm sure you'll have some bruising, but that's it. Sergeant Webber protected you well," Emma said as she put her equipment back into her black medicine bag.

"They both did."

"And it looks like Pierce is here to take even better care of you." Emma gave him a kiss on the cheek before squeezing Tammy's hand and heading over to the impatient Rose sisters.

Pierce sat down next to her and wrapped her in his arms. Tammy leaned against his chest and watched the chaos around her with absolute peace. The firefighters putting out the fires, the bomb squad and Ahmed going through the debris, and the town pushing against the barricade that had been moved closer out of fear of riot.

"Can I get you anything?" Pierce asked as he rested his chin on top of her head.

"I have everything I need right here." Tammy snuggled closer to Pierce and took a deep relaxing breath as she soaked up the warmth of his body. "How were things at the farm?"

"I don't know. I haven't been there since Friday. I'll try to get there tomorrow."

Tammy pulled away and looked at him with the confusion she felt written all over her face. "Then where were you this morning when we were calling you?"

"I was out."

For the first time, Tammy felt anger surging forward. Out? Look at him! He was looking all around at the crowd and not at her. There she was sitting on a freaking bomb and all he can say is he was out!

"Out?" She said as calmly as she could.

"Yes." Pierce stood up and nervously looked around before turning to her. "Good, it seems they're otherwise occupied. I got something for you." Pierce reached into his pocket and Tammy's eyes went wide at the bulge in his pants.

"As much as I love you, I don't know if now is the time for this," Tammy said with a blush.

"I think it's the perfect time. In fact, I can't wait a minute longer to make you mine." Tammy felt her face flame and she was about to smack him when he pulled a box out of his pocket and got down on one knee. "Tammy Elizabeth Fields, I love you and I want to spend every day for the rest of my life showing you just how much. You've brightened my life with your love and support. I would be proud to call you my wife and to share the rest of our days and nights together. Tammy, will you marry me?"

Tammy felt her body shaking with tears of happiness as he opened the box to show the perfect diamond with two pink sapphires on each side. He pulled it out of the box and held it out for her. All she had to do was say yes, but she couldn't find her voice so she just nodded and leapt into his arms.

The firefighters and bomb squad stopped to clap and the town erupted. Miss Violet thwacked a trooper on the hand with her spoon and the three Rose sisters pushed past the barricade with the trooper chasing after them until Jamison waved him off. Tammy laughed with pure joy as Pierce picked her up and spun her around before kissing her to the delight of the crowd.

CHAPTER TWENTY-THREE

Tammy joined Mrs. Davies and the women on the couch to chat happily about the wedding and babies. Emma had told her to do nothing but rest for the next week, but there was no way she was going to rest at night when Pierce was in her bed. Ever since the bomb incident the other night, Mrs. Davies, or as Tammy had been instructed, "Mom," was playing nurse. Tammy had her feet up and a pillow at her back as they all laughed at the latest gossip.

Annie and Bridget teased her about the pink pepper spray can that dangled from her key chain while Kenna, Dani, and Paige all wanted to know if there were any wedding plans. Morgan joined them and soon the discussion turned to dates, colors, and dresses until the front door banged open and Henry rushed in.

"Bless your heart, what is the matter?" Marcy jumped up as Henry was almost unrecognizable in black slacks and a red polo shirt with hardly any gel in his hair.

He looked around and zeroed in on Pierce. "You did it!" Henry ran past the ladies to where Pierce stood with the guys having a sip of bourbon in celebration of another Davies brother falling to the *M* word.

"Did what?" Pierce asked in clear confusion.

"I just got the ruling! The judge stated that the patent for the Cropbot is solely yours. Also, the media attention surrounding Dr. Oldham's death has gotten the buzz going. Everyone was wondering what the invention was. Well, they dug around the patent office and found out. It's been all over the news and I just received six offers—

all of them in the tens of millions range—for the purchase of the right to manufacture the Cropbot exclusively."

Tammy gasped and Pierce stood still just staring at Henry waving pieces of paper around like a madman. Pierce looked at her and mouthed, "Tens of millions?"

Tammy tossed back her head and laughed. Pierce ran over and scooped her off the couch and twirled her around as they laughed with all the happiness of their good fortune.

"See, I told you to drive faster! We're late and we missed something," Katelyn said as she smacked Marshall.

"Oh! It's just too much!" Marcy told them about the offers and Marshall hugged his brother and kissed Tammy's cheek before heading back over to Katelyn.

"I hope you don't mind," said Katelyn. "I brought my dad. He's just finishing up a phone call and will be in. We were over at my grandparents and he wanted to talk with Miles some," Katelyn told Marcy as Mr. Jacks entered the house.

Tammy made her way over to Ahmed and bumped against him with her shoulder. "You've been quiet." When he just looked at her, she grinned, "Okay, quieter than normal. Are you still worried about them?"

"You know I'll take care of it."

"I do. Which is the only reason I can enjoy my engagement." Tammy rose up on to her toes and kissed his cheek. "Thank you for all you do for me. And all the things I'll never even know about. You're a true friend, Ahmed." Ahmed gave a quick nod of acknowledgment, but she knew when he patted her hand that he accepted the thanks.

She smiled and headed back to where Pierce was being peppered by his sisters-in-law and friends. "We were just asking if you all had a date for the wedding in mind," Paige told her.

"We're still debating, but we're leaning toward September."

"Well, it may be too much to ask, but can it not be November?" Katelyn asked shyly.

"Why not?" Marcy asked.

"We're just going to be a little bit busy having a baby, that's all." Marshall shrugged.

"I'm three months along today!" Katelyn smiled as she patted her still-flat stomach.

"You're… Oh, Jake!!!" Marcy cried as she hugged her son and daughter-in-law.

"I know, I know, you can die happy now," Jake teased as he joined Marcy in congratulating his children.

Tammy waited as the family celebrated. She saw Ahmed look down at his phone and then quietly left. Mo smiled lovingly at Dani and rubbed her belly in such an intimate way that Tammy looked away. Pierce slid his arm around her waist and kissed her forehead as they enjoyed the celebration.

Marcy collapsed on the couch next to where Morgan and Miles sat. "Now, if only you two would give me a grandbaby soon!" she joked. Although Tammy wasn't so sure Marcy was joking.

"Only if you promise to bake me a pie a week!" Morgan teased back.

"Deal!" Marcy laughed and shook Morgan's hand.

"Great. Then I'd like my first one to be apple." The room quieted down and everyone looked at Morgan, wondering why she was carrying the joke so far. But then they looked at how Morgan and Miles were smiling at each other.

"Are you two playing a trick on me?" Marcy asked, incredulous.

"I'd never play a trick on you, Ma." Miles said with a grin, only further confusing everyone. "Morgan took the test this morning. We're going to have a baby next February!"

Ahmed stepped on to the porch and Nabi snapped to attention as he stood by the Mercedes. Cheers erupted again and he figured Morgan had just told them she was pregnant, too. John wasn't the only one in town with sources. Pain struck his heart as he remembered the son he'd only held once when he was practically a child himself. But Sergei had attacked and killed his son along with his young bride. He'd taken the only thing Ahmed had ever loved. It may have been nearly eighteen years ago, but Ahmed hadn't forgotten nor would he ever forget. He'd been hunting Sergei ever since, but had always been one step behind the allusive assassin. Sergei set himself up as an enforcer for the man in charge of the international dog-fighting ring Marshall had busted not even a year ago. Ahmed had seen Sergei's signature written all over Paul Russell's dead body. It had given him a renewed sense of vengeance. Sergei's time was running out.

"Call home and send two men to take our place. You're coming with me." Ahmed held out his hand and Nabi tossed him the keys.

"Where are we going?" Nabi asked after hanging up the phone.

"There are few things I care for in this world and someone just tried to kill one of them... twice. Where do you think we're going?" Ahmed asked menacingly.

"You found them?"

Ahmed simply looked at Nabi before accelerating faster down the country road. Of course he found them. Just like he had found where Sergei was basing his operations out of last week. No one took someone he loved from him and lived.

***

Tammy tossed her purse on the table of her apartment and smiled. In fact, she hadn't stopped smiling since she opened her eyes and saw Pierce through the smoke. "What a perfect day!"

"It was. And I was thinking about the wedding. I think we should have it at our house," Pierce said seriously.

"Honey, we don't have a house and I don't think that many people can fit in my apartment."

"Ah, we might not have one now, but we will. We have three months to build the most beautiful house for our wedding. See, I was thinking of going over those offers with Miles, Morgan, and Henry tomorrow. Give all the companies a week to submit them and then sell the manufacturing rights to the Cropbot. Then we'd have enough money to build the house of our dreams right in time for our wedding."

Tammy waved her hands in front of her face. "I've been crying way too much recently, but that's so thoughtful. But, you know, I don't care where we live. I'm perfectly happy here in this little apartment with you."

"I know. But tonight got me thinking. We don't have any room for children here." Tammy felt the tears start again but could only smile. "See, I got a spell put on me by this beautiful fairy and now all I can imagine is her as my wife and little blonde children running around the house. What do you think?"

"I think that sounds perfect." Tammy stepped into his arms and kissed him with all the love she felt. "And I think you're perfect. I love you, Pierce Davies."

"Care to show me how much?" Pierce shot her a grin that had her stripping out of her clothes and dragging him to her bed. No matter what size house they ended up having, she was keeping the tiny bed.

***

Ahmed pulled into the parking lot of the best hotel in Lexington. A valet came around to take his keys as he and Nabi stepped out of the car. He buttoned his black suit coat, walked through the glass doors and into the plush lobby.

"This is a nice place for assassins," Nabi said, looking around.

"Been to better," Ahmed shrugged. They walked to the elevator and rode in silence up to the tenth floor. "Don't say a word. You're about to see what happens when I get angry."

Ahmed walked down the hall and didn't even bother slowing down before booting his foot through the door. The door splintered off its hinges and slammed against the wall. The two men in the room were so startled that they jumped back as Ahmed walked into the room. Ahmed never pulled a weapon. He didn't need to. Sometimes things were better handled on a more personal level.

He grabbed the big one first and sent him flying against the wall. Out of the corner of his eye, he saw Nabi move to block the second man from interfering. The man Ahmed was fighting tried to fight back, but it was useless. Ahmed simply snapped his arm and threw him into the chair next to the new guy in the crew who was shaking. The little one Ahmed had shot and most likely killed had been replaced. This guy could care less about saving his partner. Partners just couldn't be depended on. That's why he worked alone.

"You will tell me everything," Ahmed said in a tone so cold the new man stopped shaking and sat there frozen in fear.

"I'm guessing you know better than that. We won't tell you a thing. And if you do kill us, that will only be the beginning. They'll just send more," the big man sneered.

"And I think you should become aware of what I am capable of so you can tell your friends." Ahmed stepped forward and grabbed the new man's hand. He shrieked as Ahmed broke finger after finger without a second's hesitation.

"Let me have one, Ahmed," Nabi whispered, too caught up in the moment to remember he was just supposed to stand there.

The big man's head snapped up. "Ahmed? *The* Ahmed?"

Ahmed stepped forward with a dangerous smile. They would pay for hurting Tammy. They would pay dearly.

Detective Basher sat at his desk. Everyone thought it would be quiet at one in the morning, though it was anything but. He shoved the papers he was looking at into a folder. He had nothing to go on for the Davies/Fields case. The room suddenly grew quiet as he looked up.

Ahmed, the head of the prince's security, was escorting two men into the room. One of them strongly resembled the sketch Pierce had given them. Of course, quite a bit more broken bones than in the sketches. Dammit. This would blow the whole case. The private security guys knew nothing!

"Detective Basher," Ahmed said in greeting as he placed two pieces of paper down in front of him. "Those are signed confessions by these men regarding the attempts on Mr. Davies and Miss Fields's lives as well as to the murder of Dr. Oldham."

"What happened to them?" Basher asked.

"We fell while trying to escape," the bigger one said.

Ahmed waited while Basher read the confessions and turned on a recorder before reading them their rights. "Are these your true and accurate confessions?" Basher waited for them to both acknowledge it. "Did you sign them under duress?"

"No," they both answered. Basher grinned and looked at Ahmed. At least he knew how to cover his tracks.

"Well, two signed confessions pretty much mean a closed case. Isn't that nice of you?" Basher said to Ahmed.

Ahmed shrugged. "I'm a nice guy." He turned and headed out the door. Sergei was next. Ahmed grinned, knowing that he had no idea of what was waiting for him.

***

Pierce stroked Tammy's hair as she slept on his chest. He felt drugged after their lovemaking and was basking in it. Slowly his eyes drifted shut as he relaxed in the night air from the open window.

The world disappeared as he was slowly transported back to the bar. He was sitting talking to the two men. "It's great that so many of your brothers played football. It's a great sport. Usually develops great men. What do your brothers do now?" the man asked Pierce. Pierce told them about his brothers and then looked at his empty glass. Since the whole bar just tilted, he figured it was time to go.

"Well, gents. It was a pleasure, but I must be getting home." Pierce stumbled off the stool and the large man caught him under the arms and held him up. The little guy rushed over and the two of them propped Pierce up.

"You aren't driving, are you?" The little responsible one asked.

"Nah. Gonna call a cab," Pierce mumbled.

"Hey. We're heading that way. Let us take you home, buddy. Then you won't have to wait forever for a cab." The men started dragging Pierce out of the bar.

"Thanks, guys. That's real nice of you all." Pierce said before passing out.

When Pierce woke up he was in the back of a car. The little guy was shaking him and Pierce opened his eyes. "Oh, good, you're awake. You were just telling us about your brothers. So, why does your brother, Cy—is that his name? Why doesn't he live in Keeneston?"

"He can live wherever he wants," Pierce commented. Hell, he didn't even know where his brother was right now.

"What does he do exactly?" The bigger man asked.

"Stuff." Pierce didn't want to talk about Cy, his absentee brother.

"Do you have his phone number? We could give him a call and ask him?" the little one suggested. Even in his drunken state, Pierce knew something was wrong. The feeling of ice-cold dread filled him.

"Nah, I don't have it. See, we don't talk. There was a big fight." Pierce pretended to pass out and let the little man shake him again.

"A fight, you say?"

"Yeah, we haven't talked in years. I don't even remember the last time he came to Keeneston. Had to be a good six, seven years ago. No one in my family talks about it, though." Pierce rolled his head and slumped back in the seat. The darkness of unconsciousness was calling to him.

"Dammit. I thought for sure he would've stayed in touch with his family," the little one said as he turned back around in his chair.

"There's a way to find out," Pierce could hear the big man say.

"What do you mean?"

"I bet he'll come home for his brother's funeral," the big man laughed.

"That would be poetic. He comes home to mourn his brother's death only to end up buried next to him the same week," the little man said as Pierce fought against the darkness seeping into his brain.

"I'll enjoy slowly torturing Cy while we question that bastard."

"Take pity on the kid here. He's already going to pay for his brother's sins so you might as well make it quick. I wonder whose car that is? 'AG DOC'. Funny license plate," the little one joked as the car came to a stop.

Pierce's eyes popped open as Tammy shook him. "Pierce! Oh, honey, you were thrashing about so much you kicked me out of bed. Shhh, it was just a bad dream," Tammy said as she stroked his hair with worry for him clear in her eyes.

Pierce gasped for air and fought the headache that came with the new memories. "It wasn't a dream. I remember. I remember everything. It was never about me. They wanted Cy. I have to warn him, he's in danger!"

###

ABOUT THE AUTHOR

Kathleen Brooks is the bestselling author of the Bluegrass Series. She has garnered attention as a new voice in romance with a warm Southern feel. Her books feature quirky small town characters you'll feel like you've known forever, romance, humor, and mystery all mixed into one perfect glass of sweet tea.

Kathleen is an animal lover who supports rescue organizations and other non-profit organizations whose goals are to protect and save our four-legged family members.

Kathleen lives in Central Kentucky with her husband, daughter, two dogs, and a cat who thinks he's a dog. She loves to hear from readers and can be reached at Kathleen@Kathleen-Brooks.com

Check out the Website for updates on the Bluegrass Series. You can also "Like" Kathleen on Facebook and follow her on Twitter @BluegrassBrooks.

Other Books by Kathleen Brooks

Bluegrass Brothers Series Continues!

The fifth and final book in the Bluegrass Brothers Series will be out in the Fall of 2013. Be sure to like me on Facebook or follow my Blog to get updates on the release date!

The mysterious Cy Davies is coming home. He's not coming alone either. Having rescued Gemma Perry, a sassy investigative reporter for a gossip magazine, he takes her to the one place he knows he can keep her safe. Keeneston.

Gemma Perry was having a bad week. Now she was in a small town where gossip was a currency. She should fit right in, except for the fact that she unwillingly holds the secret to bring down an internationally wanted man who is sparing no expense to keep those secrets safe.

And I just couldn't leave Keeneston without a proper finale. Ahmed will be getting a book too! Ahmed's book is scheduled for release in early 2014. More details will come soon.

Bluegrass Series

Bluegrass State of Mind

McKenna Mason, a New York City attorney with a love of all things Prada, is on the run from a group of powerful, dangerous men. McKenna turns to a teenage crush, Will Ashton, for help in starting a new life in beautiful horse country. She finds that Will is now a handsome, successful race horse farm owner. As the old flame is ignited, complications are aplenty in the form of a nasty ex-wife, an ex-boyfriend intent on killing her, and a feisty race horse who refuses to race without a kiss. Can Will and McKenna cross the finish line together, and more importantly, alive?

Risky Shot

Danielle De Luca, an ex-beauty queen who is not at all what she seems, leaves the streets of New York after tracking the criminals out to destroy her. She travels to Keeneston, Kentucky, to make her final stand by the side of her best friend McKenna Mason. While in Keeneston, Danielle meets the quiet and mysterious Mohtadi Ali Rahmen, a modern day prince. Can Mo protect Dani from the group of powerful men in New York? Or will Dani save the prince from his rigid, loveless destiny?

Dead Heat

In the third book of the Bluegrass Series, Paige Davies finds her world turned upside down as she becomes involved in her best friend's nightmare. The strong-willed Paige doesn't know which is worse: someone trying to kill her, or losing her dog to the man she loves to hate.

FBI Agent Cole Parker can't decide whether he should strangle or kiss this infuriating woman of his dreams. As he works the case of his career, he finds that love can be tougher than bringing down some of the most powerful men in America.

***

Bluegrass Brothers Series

Bluegrass Undercover

Cade Davies had too much on his plate to pay attention to newest resident of Keeneston. He was too busy avoiding the Davies Brothers marriage trap set by half the town. But when a curvy redhead lands in Keeneston, the retired Army Ranger finds himself drawn to her. These feelings are only fueled by her apparent indifference and lack of faith in his ability to defend himself.

DEA Agent Annie Blake was undercover to bust a drug ring hiding in the adorable Southern town that preyed on high school athletes. She had thought to keep her head down and listen to the local gossip to find the maker of this deadly drug. What Annie didn't count on was becoming the local gossip. With marriage bets being placed, and an entire town aiming to win the pot, Annie looks to Cade for help in bringing down the drug ring before another kid is killed. But can she deal with the feelings that follow?

Rising Storm

Katelyn Jacks was used to being front and center as a model. But she never had to confront the Keeneston Grapevine! After retiring from the runway and returning to town to open a new animal clinic, Katelyn found that her life in the public eye was anything but over. While working hard to establish herself as the new veterinarian in town, Katelyn finds her life uprooted by a storm of love, gossip, and a vicious group of criminals.

Marshall Davies is the new Sheriff in Keeneston. He is also right at the top of the town's most eligible bachelor list. His affinity for teasing the hot new veterinarian in town has led to a rush of emotions that he wasn't ready for. Marshall finds his easy days of breaking up fights at the local PTA meetings are over when he and Katelyn discover that a dog-fighting ring has stormed into their normally idyllic town. As their love struggles to break through, they must battle to save the lives of the dogs and each other.

Acquiring Trouble

As a natural born leader, Miles Davies accomplishes anything he puts his mind to. Upon returning home from his special forces duties, he has become the strong foundation of the Davies family and his company. But that strong foundation is about to get rocked in a big way by the one woman that always left him fascinated and infuriated.

Keeneston's notorious bad girl is back! Morgan Hamilton's life ended and began on her high school graduation night when she left Keeneston with no plan to ever return. As a self-made businesswoman, Morgan is always looking for her next victory. Little did she know that next victory would involve acquiring the company that belonged to the one man she always wanted for herself.

With their careers and lives on the line, will Miles and Morgan choose love or ambition?

Make sure you don't miss each new book as they are published. Sign up email notification of all new releases at **http://www.Kathleen-Brooks.com**.

Printed in Great Britain
by Amazon